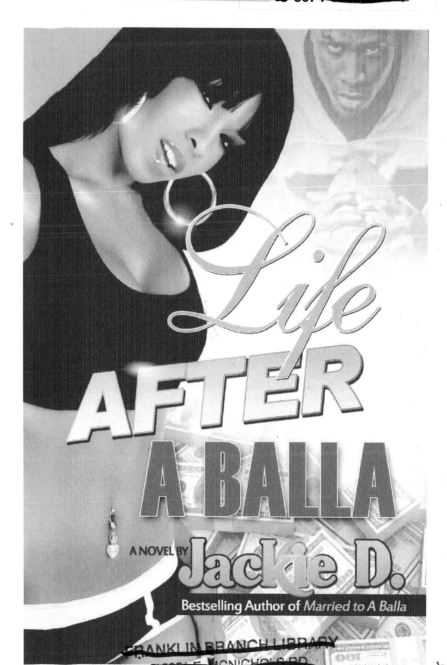

Life AFTER A BALLA

A NOVEL BY **Jackie D.**

Bestselling Author of *Married to A Balla*

Life
AFTER
A BALLA

A NOVEL BY
Jackie D.

Life Changing Books in conjunction with Power Play Media
Published by Life Changing Books
P.O. Box 423 Brandywine, MD 20613

Library of Congress Cataloging-in-Publication Data;

www.lifechangingbooks.net
13 Digit: 978-1934230374
10 Digit: 1-934230375

Dedication

This book is dedicated to Leslie Allen, the best editor/operations manager in the entire world. As I said before...words can not express how much I appreciate you. You only cursed me out once during this project when it should've been many more. LOL! You knew I had a lot on my plate this time, so thank you for being so understanding and for all of your help.

Also...to my one and only son, Emanuel "Poobie" Chapman, III...I love you boy!!

Acknowledgments

To all my friends and family, thanks for the love and support! To Azarel, thanks again for allowing me to publish another book with such a wonderful group of people. You're the best! To all my fellow LCB Authors, Danette Majette (my BFF for life), Tiphani Montgomery, Tonya Ridley, CJ Hudson, J.Tremble, Ms. KP, Carla Pennington, VegasClarke, Kendall Banks, Capone, Mike Warren, Chris Renee, and any one else on the team that I missed. LCB FOR LIFE!!

To Joy Avery, thanks for everything. A special thanks to all the distributors and independent book stores that helped promote my books; The Literary Joint locations, The Urban Knowledge locations, DC Book Diva, The Books-A-Million locations that are still open, Black and Nobel in Philly, Novel Tee's and the rest of the book stores that showed me love. Thank you.

To the test readers Ashundria and Tasha, thank you so much for your input. Last but not least...To all the people that purchased this book as well as my other two, I really appreciate all the positive messages on Facebook and Twitter expressing how much you loved reading my work. From the bottom of my heart, thank you!

Check me out at
http:// www.facebook.com/loveheist
twitter.com/therealjackied

Peace and Blessings,
Jackie D.

Chapter One

"Didn't I tell you bitch...till death do us part!" Sandino roared in Skye's ear. He grabbed the back of her head and rammed her face into the head board.

"I'm sorry, Sandino please stop," Skye pleaded in pain as blood from her busted nose trickled down the right side of her face.

"It's too late for apologies. I told you if you ever left me I would kill you," he said, ripping her panties off and pinning her arms above her head. "And then you go fuck some other nigga!"

Skye screamed in horror when she felt excruciating pain between her legs. She wondered what type of object Sandino was raping her with as he became more and more aggressive. When she felt something running down her legs, she lifted her head and looked down. Her eyes widened when she saw a huge puddle of blood on the sheets and Sandino holding her son's basketball trophy covered in blood. She became hysterical and tried to kick him off the bed, but he didn't budge. She was no match for Sandino's muscular frame.

He gave her an evil glare then started yelling once again.

"This will teach your ass for givin' my pussy away!" he yelled, shoving the trophy inside her again. "Here I was searchin' for you and my kids while your ass was out fuckin' another dude."

"Please stop…you're hurting me," Skye pleaded as tears immediately began to stream down her face. "I promise…I didn't sleep with anyone else!"

"Stop lyin' bitch, I can tell when somebody's been in my pussy," Sandino belted, then rammed the trophy again. "You were with that nigga, Justice!"

The pain was excruciating. "Sandino, I haven't been with anyone but you!"

"Shut the fuck up!"

When Skye saw Sandino attempting to push the trophy inside her once again, she started screaming and pounding him in the chest. Laughing, Sandino dropped the trophy, but instead of stopping, he attacked her again, delivering a quick hard blow to her abdomen.

"That shit was for me having to look for your ass when you left me!"

Skye screamed out in pain and curled up in the fetal position, but he wasn't finished. Moments later, Sandino grabbed Skye by her hair, dragged her off the bed and swung her body up against the wall like a rag doll.

"And that was for me getting shot!"

Completely hysterical and bleeding, Skye attempted to crawl on all fours trying to make it to the door when suddenly she felt a plastic bag over her head. Panic-stricken, she immediately started gasping for air, squirming and grabbing at his hands. She couldn't breathe. It felt like she was suffocating. This was not the way she wanted to die. She started grabbing for the bag, but just couldn't seem to get a grip. It felt like she was slipping into unconsciousness.

"Noooo!" Skye yelled out as all three of her kids faces flashed before her eyes.

Suddenly, someone started tugging on her right shoulder. "Skye, wake up," she heard a male voice say.

When Skye slowly opened her eyes, she was still clawing at her neck. With her heart racing, it felt like she was seconds away from a heart attack.

"Baby, are you okay?" Cruze asked in his raspy voice trying to comfort her. She was relieved to see her handsome boyfriend as he leaned over and placed his arm around her. At that moment, Skye realized she'd fallen asleep on the plane. "I guess you had another nightmare, huh?"

Skye covered the lower half of her face then shook her head back and forth. She was still shaking and the palm of her hands were soaking wet.

"Damn, it seemed so real, like he was really trying to kill me. I thought these nightmares were a thing of the past."

"Yeah, me, too," Cruze agreed. "You haven't had one in weeks."

"This trip back to Miami must've triggered them again." Skye went into her purse and pulled out her Ativan. For the past eight months, she'd been on the medication that was prescribed to control her panic attacks.

"I know you've been through a lot, but I'll be glad when you get off that shit," Cruze replied with a concerned tone. "I told you I looked it up on the internet. Ativan can be highly addictive."

Instead of responding, Skye continued to turn the top on the prescription bottle. A few seconds later a male flight attendant walked over. He was tall, about 6'3, and obviously gay by the way he switched over wearing a ton of foundation, heavy eye liner and clear lip gloss. His long hair was pulled back into a ponytail and his uniform was way too tight.

"Excuse me. Is everything alright?" he asked after hearing the commotion.

"Yes, she's fine. Can you bring her something to drink?" Cruze answered.

The flight attendant stared at Skye for a second with his hand on his hip. "That type of disturbance can alarm the other

3

passengers. Are you sure everything is okay?"

Cruze turned and looked at him with an attitude. "Look, RuPaul, I told you she was good, now can you please go do your job."

It looked as if the flight attendant wanted to come back with some type of catty response, but instead he rolled his eyes and sashayed away.

Cruze looked over at Skye. "How much longer can we keep this up? I'll be so glad when you divorce Sandino's ass and put the past behind you for good. It's been almost a year and a half since you left him. You were just starting to be yourself again, smiling, happy and enjoying life. Now, Sandino and his bullshit ass lawyer are trying to pull you back into the madness. I refuse to let anyone hurt you again," he said, squeezing her tight. *I still can't believe that muthafucka didn't die the night I shot him,* Cruze thought.

It came to a complete surprise to everyone that Sandino had managed to survive a gunshot wound to the back of his head. With the amount of blood he'd lost, they assumed he was dead that night. That is until the paramedics rushed in and announced that he still had a pulse. They later found out that he had surgery and survived. Keeping up with his condition had become top priority to both Cruze and Skye. They wanted him dead, he needed to be stopped but Sandino had proved once again that he wasn't going anywhere.

Cruze rubbed Skye's arm delicately. "I love you so much."

When Skye looked at Cruze her heart fluttered. She loved the way his big arms felt around her because he made her feel so safe. She grabbed one if his dreads and twirled it around her fingers. They were growing really fast. Although he'd picked up weight and didn't have the once rock hard one hundred and eighty pound body, Skye still found him irresistible. But who was she to talk. She no longer had her toned one hundred thirty five pound body either. All the good eating and loving contributed to both of their weight gain. Luckily she'd gained it in all the right places so she still was able to turn heads whenever she entered a room.

"Are you sure you up to this meeting?" Cruze asked.

Skye could still remember the first time she received the phone call from Sandino's lawyer's relentless assistant. Every time the assistant called she insisted that Skye meet with Sandino's lawyer to discuss a very important matter, one that couldn't be discussed over the phone.

What the hell was so important that it couldn't be discussed over the phone, Skye wondered.

The thought made her nervous. She should've followed her first instinct and not come at all, but she felt she had to. If for nothing else, to strangle the assistant for calling her every day for a month straight. Skye never once talked to Sandino's lawyer, which seemed quite odd.

"I might as well get the shit over with. I wonder how they even got my damn number? I have to admit though. I do have some concerns." Skye lowered her voice to make sure no one could hear what she was about to say. "What if this meeting is because they suspect that Sandino didn't really come to my apartment that night threatening to commit suicide? What if they don't believe that when Kareem and I tried to stop him the gun accidently went off? What if they try to charge me with attempted murder? This could be a set up," Skye whispered.

"Lawyer's are crooked as hell. They have ways of getting phone numbers. Baby just relax, the way we decided to cover everything up that night already convinced the police months ago," Cruze whispered as well. "They have no idea that I shot Sandino, got rid of Justice's body or was even in your apartment that night. If that was the case, the police would be calling you, not his lawyer. Everything will be alright, trust me," he reassured her.

Thoughts of how Cruze and Kareem had thrown Jus-

5

tice's body out the back of Skye's first floor bedroom window, then managed to get the corpse into the car without being seen still shocked him. If Skye had lived in a more upscale neighborhood and the police would've arrived in a more timely manner, things may not have gone so smoothly. Even the neighbors didn't come outside until the police arrived.

"Are you sure no one saw you that night? You know...putting Justice in the car?"

Cruze shrugged his shoulders. "I guess not. But even if they did, you know the code in the hood. No snitching."

"I just wish Sandino had died and wasn't still hanging on in some damn rehab center. Sometimes I feel like that man will always be a thorn in my side," Skye said.

"Not as long as I'm here, he won't be. I should've never stood back all those years without helping you. That's why I shot him that night he came after you. I couldn't let him hurt you and the kids anymore. But let's forget about that night. We're moving forward," Cruze said, kissing her on the lips.

Skye forced a smile even though she was still concerned.

"I gotta go piss. I hope I see that punk ass flight attendant who still hasn't bought you the drink I asked for." Cruze unbuckled his seat beat and headed towards the back of the plane.

Skye didn't even have time to be with her own thoughts before realizing the older lady sitting in the aisle across from her was staring a little too hard.

"That's why I always take me a sip or two before I fly to calm my nerves. Just pray and ask God to get rid of those demons in your dreams. I've been watching you, and trust me when I tell you this, God has a plan for you," the woman advised.

Skye smiled at the lady, who was dressed in an expensive suit and also had an old vintage Chanel bag clinched tightly in her lap. She missed buying all the new designer bags before they hit the stores. But she could only reminisce about shopping now. Her days of going to the rack and grabbing what she wanted without even looking at the price tag was now replaced with looking for the rack with the bright red sale or clearance sign on it.

But, I did what I needed to do to have a better life for my family, so I'm not going to get emotional over material things, she thought.

Skye was determined that nothing or no one was ever going to send her back to that dark place she'd come out of just eight months ago. She was deeply depressed from the betrayal of her ex-boyfriend, Justice Mitchell, the man she thought really loved her. Not only did she find out he was married, but the fact that he led Sandino to her apartment that dreadful night was even worse. Thinking back to the horrible incident once again, Skye still couldn't believe that Justice had been killed. She trusted him, but felt as though he'd gotten what he deserved after leading Sandino to her just for the money.

She remembered how her, Cruze and Kareem frantically ran around the apartment getting rid of the evidence that night after Justice and Sandino got shot. They were shocked when Jordan, who was over at the neighbor's house came running inside the apartment. He was frightened and yelling that he'd called 911 after looking out the window and seeing his father in the parking lot. At that moment they realized they didn't have time to get rid of Sandino's body. That's when they decided to come up with the plan that Sandino came over in a rage threatening to kill himself. Cruze then fled the scene to get rid of Justice's body just in the nick of time.

After she was continuously interrogated by the police and harassed by the press who posted up outside her home hours later, Skye and the kids eventually moved from Marietta to another small town outside of Atlanta called Lawrenceville.

LIFE *After* A BALLA

She could no longer stay in that apartment where everything had taken place. She also cut herself off from the world refusing to deal with anybody or take any phone calls. At the time, it was just too much for her to bear. She became distant from her own kids, stayed in her room for days and just cried. She even tried to get a job shortly after the shootings to get her mind off of things, but she couldn't focus and eventually got fired. Thank God Cruze stayed around to help out and paid the rent so her kids could continue to have a roof over their heads.

After Skye got herself together and things calmed down, Cruze confessed his love for her. It took a while for him to win her over though because she didn't trust men anymore. She was very hesitant about going into another relationship, but the whole ordeal with Sandino that night made Skye and Cruze form a bond. After all, he wasn't a stranger. He'd been Sandino's best friend for years, and always wanted her to be happy.

Skye had to admit, she'd always been attracted to Cruze, but knew Sandino would've killed her if he ever found out. After two months of Cruze confessing his love for her and the kids, Skye finally gave in, but told him that before they could even talk about being together he had to give up the streets. She didn't want to deal with the drama or risk him getting locked up or even killed. He agreed, and although money was tight for once in her life she was truly happy.

Skye stopped reminiscing when she saw Cruze coming back down the aisle with a Sprite in his hand. When he sat down, she immediately popped her two pills and tried to relax. She definitely felt uneasy about this trip back to Miami, and hoped that whatever the meeting was about didn't get her even more upset.

Once they landed an hour later, Skye didn't waste anytime grabbing her purse and heading towards the front of the plane. When they passed the gay flight attendant, he was standing in the doorway with his arms folded and his nose turned up. While Cruze laughed, Skye didn't pay the homosexual man any attention. She was too nervous about the meeting to be worried about some gay dude with an attitude.

While walking though the busy Miami International Airport, as soon as Skye saw the sign for the La Caireta Restaurant in Terminal D, it immediately bought back memories of her and Asia. Stopping to get a bite to eat at that restaurant was their ritual before taking the trips she used to sneak with Asia while Sandino was away at training camp. Anger suddenly came over her when she thought of her once best friend.

To think I trusted her, and she disappeared with all my money. She better hope I never see her again. I definitely have something in mind for that bitch if I do. Now, I have to go deal with this damn lawyer. I hope he don't piss me off because I will turn that muthafucking office out if I have to.

LIFE *After* A BALLA

Chapter Two

Skye squinted her eyes from the bright Miami sun as they headed outside and flagged down a cab. After reaching in her purse and pulling out a new pair of knock off Gucci sunglasses, she watched as several expensive cars rode by. When Skye spotted a silver Aston Martin Roadster with twenty-two inch Forgiato rims pull up to the curb, she thought, *Yeah, I'm definitely back in MIA.* In the town she lived in now, two-hundred thousand dollar cars were non-existent. Looking at all the rich, tanned people, it made Skye somewhat envious. She had to admit, she missed the sun.

When the cab pulled up a few seconds later both she and Cruze hopped inside. They had a few hours to spare before Skye had to go to meet Sandino's lawyer.

"11 Washington Avenue Miami Beach," Cruze instructed the driver.

Skye looked over at him with a huge grin on her face, she immediately recognized the street.

"Don't tell me we're going to my favorite spot?"

"Yep. I know how much you love Joe's Stone Crab. Besides, you can't go into a meeting on an empty stomach. You barely ate breakfast before we left Georgia."

"You always know exactly what to do to make me smile," Skye said, kissing Cruze on his lips. "Can you afford this though? I know it's been a while since you sold a car, and you just bought me that Michelle watch. With our bills…"

"Sssssh. Don't worry about that. I told you I got you, babe," he interrupted.

Even though Cruze had promised to stay out the streets, he lied. Skye assumed the little bit of money he had coming in was from his job as a car salesman at some mom and pop car lot. Instead, Cruze was back in the streets selling drugs again. Even though he knew it was wrong, and wanted to abide by Skye's rules, in his mind he had to make some real money in order to provide Skye with the lifestyle she was accustomed to. He knew Skye didn't want anything from him, but he wanted to spoil her by giving her nice things. Plus, what she didn't know was that Cruze just wasn't a nine to five type of guy. He was married to the streets.

As they laughed and talked all the way to the restaurant, Skye thought this was the perfect opportunity to finally tell Cruze her good news. She reached inside her purse and pulled out some paperwork and handed it to him.

"I did this a few weeks after the incident," she advised.

After looking at the paper, it only took a few seconds before a huge smile appeared across his face. It was Skye's divorce papers.

"Since I'm going to see Sandino's lawyer, I might as well hand him the papers so they can deliver them to his crazy ass."

Cruze was so excited, he was glad she was finally closing that chapter of her life. He clapped his hands together and looked up towards the sky like he was saying a prayer. "Damn, you had a nigga speechless for a minute. I almost stuck my head out the window and yelled to the top of my lungs with that news. All this time I've been preaching to you about moving on with your life and you'd already filed for divorce. Now that's what I'm talking bout baby," he said, leaning over and kissing her cheek.

"Yeah, I've been waiting for this moment for a while."

"Shit, me, too," he co-signed.

"Maybe when the divorce is final I can finally get some damn alimony or even some child support."

Cruze looked at her sideways. "Is that one of the reasons why you finally filed? We don't need his money."

The last thing Skye wanted was to make him upset. "No, that's not one of the reasons why I filed. I filed because I need to finally be rid of him. But don't you think I deserve to still live a good life after all he put me and my kids through? Plus, you wouldn't have to work as hard."

"Well, that's what I'm here for, to take care of you guys."

Cruze's overprotective ways was one of the main reasons why Skye had fallen for him.

"You always know just what to say," Skye beamed.

Twenty minutes later, they pulled up in front of the restaurant. As Skye looked up at the sign, memories of how her family use to frequent the establishment before Sandino lost his mind flooded her thoughts. She also remembered that a lot of the Miami Dolphin players and their families used to eat there as well.

I hope I don't run into any of them, I'm not in the mood for no fake conversation, she thought.

After making their way inside, several men almost broke their necks looking at Skye. Although she'd picked up a little weight and was wearing a conservative black suit, she still seemed to mesmerize men with her beauty as they waited to be seated.

Cruze glared back at the staring men. He then walked behind Skye and began massaging her shoulders.

"Ahhh, that feels good," she moaned.

"I want you to relax and enjoy lunch before the meeting. No stressing," he advised.

Jackie D.

"Okay, no stressing."

A few minutes later the hostess came and led them to a table. Once they were seated, Skye began to look over the menu.

"I sure don't wanna meet the lawyer smelling like seafood, but I'm about to get my grub on," she informed. "It's been so long since I've had Joe's."

"Do your thing, baby. That's what we're here for," Cruze said with a slight grin.

At that moment, the waitress walked over to the table. "Hello, welcome to Joe's Stone Crab. My name is Natalie and I'll be your server. Can I start you two off with something to drink?" she looked back and forth from Skye to Cruze.

"Actually, I'm ready to order," Skye responded.

The waitress smiled and pulled out her pad. "I guess someone's hungry. Go ahead."

"I'll have the Maine Lobster Tail with crab cake stuffing," Skye spoke.

"And I'll have the Jumbo Lumb crab cakes with green tomatoes," Cruze added.

"Would either of you like anything from the bar?" the waitress asked.

"I'll have a Hennessey and Coke," Cruze responded.

"Just a Coke for me," Skye said.

"Okay, I'll be right back," the waitress said, walking away.

Skye looked around. The place looked different. The ambiance was very romantic. There were white candles and crisp white table cloths. They even had fresh cut roses as center pieces on each table.

A few minutes later, the waitress bought their drinks.

"Here's to a new life with no more worries," Cruze said, raising his glass for a toast.

Skye grabbed her glass and smiled as they clinked their glasses together. "I'll definitely drink to that," Skye said, tak-

Jackie D.

ing a sip of her coke and gazing into Cruze's eyes as they sparkled mischievously. Something serious, yet erotic always seemed to be going on in his eyes when he looked at her.

Their gazes caught and held for a few minutes. While Skye bit down on her lip and started twirling her hair, Cruze stuck out his huge tongue, moving it in a circular motion along his lips. Their chemistry was crazy and they loved having sex with each other.

"Damn, I wanna fuck the shit out of you right now," Cruze said.

Skye looked around the restaurant then towards the restrooms. "You know you can get it right here baby."

Cruze displayed a massive smile. "Are you serious?"

As soon as she gave him the signal, they both got up and headed to the restroom area. Skye looked over her shoulder before entering the men's bathroom to make sure nobody was watching. When the coast was clear she walked behind Cruze into the stall closing the door behind them.

They immediately started kissing while he unzipped her pants pulling them to her knees. Skye could feel the passion building inside of her. Cruze quickly pulled down his pants and turned her around so she was facing the stall door.

"This is just a quickie baby, but tonight I want to taste my pussy and you already know I'm going to make you cum all night," he whispered in a raw and sexy tone in her ear.

Skye knew he was telling the truth, his head game was something she'd never experienced in her life. The multiple orgasms from his huge, thick tongue were priceless. Her pussy was getting wet just thinking about it.

This man is trying to drive me crazy, Skye thought to herself.

As Cruze slid his thickness inside her from behind she bent over and arched her back. He adjusted himself and started thrusting strong and deep. He started out with a slow rhythm, but it quickly turned into a faster more satisfying thrust send-

15

ing sensations and fire throughout her body.

"Baby, you feel so good," she said, as he rode her ass deep and hard.

"You feel good, too. Don't ever take this pussy away from me," he moaned.

Their pulsating rhythm and the way Skye stuck her ass out throwing the pussy and giving him full access drove Cruze insane. Seconds later, he felt himself about to cum as he rode her ass pounding it repeatedly.

In a strangled voice, he asked, "You gonna cum with me, baby?"

"Yes," she whispered.

"I want to feel it on my dick." Skye's pussy muscles suddenly contracted. "Yeah baby, I feel it, cum for me," Cruze said.

Her legs started to tremble as Skye's orgasm approached. "Oh shit," she said, breathing uncontrollably.

Cruze released a deep moan as he wrapped his hands around her waist and dug inside her harder and faster. Seconds later he released.

"I love you, Skye," he whispered in her ear.

"I love you, too."

Several hours later, Skye looked out the back window of the cab at the rows of beautiful palm trees while making her way toward the financial district in the heart of downtown. Being back in *The Magic City* Skye realized she truly missed portions of her old life. The only thing she didn't miss was getting her ass beat by Sandino on a daily basis and dealing with all his hoe's trying to disrespect her.

After arriving at Sandino's lawyer's office, Cruze decided not to join the meeting so Skye could have her space. Not to mention, he was afraid that he might hear something to

Jackie D.

set him off. Cruze knew Sandino well enough to know he would always try to control or have the upper hand on Skye whether he was alive, in the hospital or dead. He just hoped Skye was prepared, because without a doubt, Sandino always had a hidden agenda.

Cruze decided to go across the street to the Sports Bar he saw when they pulled up. As soon as he entered, he saw a crazy looking woman sitting at the bar staring at him like he was a piece of meat. He walked to the opposite side hoping that she caught the hint that he didn't want to be bothered. He sat down and told the bartender he wanted a Hennessey and Coke. The bartender nodded his head and reached under the bar pulling out a tiny glass. The woman obviously didn't catch the hint as she headed over and sat beside him.

"Damn, you're the best thing I've seen all day. I need to take you home," she said with a huge smile.

It never seized to amaze Cruze just how forward the Miami women could be. He didn't respond but was glad when the bartender came over with his drink.

"That'll be ten dollars," the bartender said.

Damn, for that little ass drink, Cruze thought as he reached inside his pocket and pulled out the money.

"Cat got your tongue good looking," the woman said, attempting to reach over and grab one of his dreads.

Cruze caught her hand and pushed it away.

"I'm not interested," he told her and smoothly slid off the bar stool leaving her sitting there.

"Well, fuck you then. Your ass must be gay or one of those down low brothers," she stated loudly.

"I think you've had enough to drink," the bartender said to her.

"Mannnn, fuck you, too," the woman spat, getting up from the bar. She took two steps and fell flat on her face causing the dingy red dress she was wearing to fly up above her waist.

17

Jackie D.

Cruze turned his head when he realized she didn't have any panties on. He couldn't help but laugh at the woman as she got up and staggered out the door a few seconds later.

"You probably shoulda called her a cab," Cruze told the bartender.

"She lives two blocks away, so she'll be alright. I deal with her ass almost every night."

Cruze shook his head and ordered several more drinks. While sipping, he sat thinking about how he sometimes felt bad about betraying his once best friend by shooting him and falling in love with his wife. But then again, he would always think back to how Sandino started treating all the people who really loved him. Sandino seemed to forget that Cruze was the one in the streets making all the money back in the day and helped Sandino while he was in college. Once Sandino left home for school, Cruze made sure that he never had to go back to his dysfunctional home life, which included his drug addicted mother Peaches. Cruze took care of Sandino, buying him clothes and giving him money. They were like brothers. When Sandino got signed to the NFL, he promised Cruze that he would return the favor and take care of him, but the money, fame and drugs changed him. It always puzzled Cruze why Sandino didn't appreciate what he had, a beautiful wife and three wonderful kids, and a best friend who would've had his back no matter what. Sandino even turned his back on Cruze when he got into some trouble and spent a short time in prison.

That nigga definitely got some fucked up ways, Cruze thought. *He turned his back on me way too many times, but that's okay though. I got something out of the deal that could never be replaced.*

For the first time in his life, he was in love. No other woman could even make him cheat on Skye. In fact he'd cut all of them off. Skye completed him, so Cruze knew in his heart she was the one. He even wanted to marry her one day, which was why he constantly pushed the divorce issue. He also had plans of talking Skye into having his child since he didn't have any kids. Cruze was in it for the long haul. However, he knew that there was one small issue. If Skye knew he was back in the streets she would be pissed. Cruze didn't like keeping secrets from her, and even though he was doing this for them, for now, he had to make sure she didn't find out he was involved in any illegal activities.

"I'm not gonna lose her like Sandino did," he said to himself.

A few seconds later his attention was directed to one of the large flat screen televisions on the wall. It was an important news break about a bank robbery gone bad and the two suspects were shot dead by police. Cruze almost jumped out his seat when one of the suspects was Sandino's boy, Black.

Damn, Black, what the hell you doing robbing banks? I guess not having Sandino and being strung out on that shit finally caught up to your ass, Cruze thought taking his drink to the head.

Cruze was on his fourth drink when his phone rang, thinking it might be Skye telling him she was finished he glanced at his phone. Realizing it was the business call he'd been waiting on, he quickly answered.

"Yo, what up Duke?"

"What up, nigga," Duke responded.

"I'm at the Bleu Moon Sports Bar downtown on Bayshore Drive. Can you be here in like twenty minutes? I know how you're always late, nigga. I don't have all day to wait."

"Be easy, man. I'm on my way," Duke said ending the call.

Now that he was back in the streets getting money, he didn't like dealing with dudes in Georgia. He preferred to deal with the connect he'd met in Miami years ago. Not to mention, Miami had some of the best coke in the world.

Cruze tapped the huge bulge of money in his pocket

Jackie D.

that Skye and even TSA had managed not to catch onto. *I wonder how Skye is going to react when I tell her we have to drive back to Georgia instead of flying.*

Chapter Three

Skye sat for what seemed like thirty minutes twiddling her thumbs looking out of the huge glass window inside the conference room. She looked around admiring the décor. The huge black oval conference table had small marble specks that matched the high-back leather chairs. The trendy room had a calm and private ambience. Skye especially liked the well-crafted wooden floors. They added to the overall look and feel of the room. Looking at the sign on the wall that read, *Toni Vaughn and Associates*, Skye had heard the name often, and knew the top notch lawyer definitely came highly recommended in the Miami area.

Tired of flipping through the outdated magazines, her mind drifted to what the woman on the plane said to her. "God has a plan for you."

As the statement replayed over and over in her mind, Skye wondered what the plan was.

Moments later, a woman rushed into the conference room and threw her gold Louis Vuitton Alma bag on the table. When she walked over and apologized for being late, then introduced herself, Skye was totally shocked, to see that Toni Vaughn was actually a female. She expected to see some white stuck up lawyer wearing a boring grey suit come in carrying a worn down leather briefcase. Instead, she was exchanging a handshake with a well respected black female sports attorney who represented several NFL players. Toni was a beautiful woman, with a gorgeous mocha complexion, and long chocolate brown hair that was pulled back in a neat ponytail. Skye admired her well-fit Marc Jacobs pant suit and Sergio Rossi peep-toe pumps. Now, it made perfect sense why Sandino never bothered to introduce them. Skye couldn't help but wonder if the two of them had ever fucked.

Knowing him, I'm sure they did, she thought.

"It's good to finally meet you, Ms. Vaughn," Skye stated with a suspicious glare.

"Nice to finally meet you, too, Mrs. Washington. I can't believe I've been representing Sandino all this time, and we've never met. Oh, by the way, call me Toni."

"And you can call me, Skye. I no longer wanna go by Mrs. Washington."

Toni gave Skye a questionable look. "Will do."

The two immediately got better acquainted by Toni asking about Skye and the kids well-being. Once that small talk was out of the way, Toni then decided to ask Skye if she knew anything about Sandino's condition. When Skye told her that she refused to look at the news or listen to anything dealing with his shooting, Toni decided it was time to bring her up to speed on Sandino's prognosis. She looked at Skye funny, wondering why she didn't know what was going on with her own husband.

"So, you don't know anything? It's been back and forth on the news since the day it happened," Toni mentioned.

"Listen Toni, let me explain something to you. I went through a traumatic experience at the hands of that man. He abused me for years and I'd finally left him and moved away. He found us and came to my house with a gun trying to kill himself. Since that night, I've been having trouble sleeping and been taking medication all because of him. I didn't want to know anything about his condition. I just wanted to move on with my life and try to get over the pain I endured all these years. But if you feel it's necessary to discuss, go ahead," Skye said.

"Well, let's start at the beginning, I guess," Toni said, sitting down. "I believe it's still amazing to everybody how Sandino survived this type of gunshot wound. I still find it hard to believe that he came to your home threatening to kill himself. It seems so unlike him."

Suddenly, Skye became a bit nervous, but tried to play it off. "Well, Toni I'm sure there's a lot about my husband that you will never know. He wasn't exactly the man everyone thought he was."

Hearing the tone in Skye's voice told Toni not to touch the obviously sensitive subject.

"From what I've been told the bullet passed through his head without crossing the midline of the brain, where the most critical injuries typically result. The penetration was nearly fatal, and he's lucky. After finding out that your son was the one who called 911, he actually saved his life. If Sandino hadn't gotten to the hospital just in time, he surely would've died."

Skye sat listening to Toni thinking, *yeah…yeah…yeah, I already know all this shit. I had to keep up with his progress to make sure he wasn't coming after me again or telling the police the truth. I know that after the doctor's performed an emergency surgery to extract skull fragments and a small amount of tissue from his brain, and that part of his skull was removed to avoid further damage. Shit it's because of that surgery that saved his sorry ass life. They should'a let 'em die.*

After the surgery, Sandino was placed in a medically induced coma to allow his brain to rest. Surprisingly he ended up beating the odds by surviving several life threatening infections and later started making progress towards recovery. Four months later, he was transferred to one of the best rehabilitations centers in Miami.

Skye continued listening to Toni as if the information was all new to her.

"One of the first steps in Sandino's rehabilitation is to help him try and regain the ability to take care of himself. Although he's made some amazing progress, the brain injury did cause paralysis on the left side of his body and severe memory loss. The right side of his body doesn't respond well either, so he's taking occupational and physical therapy and he's also working with a speech therapist." Toni explained.

Skye was relieved to find out that Sandino had a lack of memory. "So, can he talk?"

Toni shook her head. "Not that well. He mostly mumbles things, but he can manage to say yes and no every once in a while."

At that moment, Skye reached inside her purse deciding this was the perfect time to give Toni the divorce papers. When she slid them across the table, Toni looked at the papers then back at Skye.

"I think you might wanna hold off on this until you hear what I have to say," Toni replied.

Suddenly, their conversation was interrupted by Toni's assistant knocking on the door. "Excuse me Ms. Vaughn, I just wanted to remind you about your 2:00."

Toni looked at her watch realizing she was running behind. "Okay, Erin thank you."

"Alright Skye since we need to wrap things up, I'll start off by telling you, I have some good news and some bad news to discuss. Which do you prefer to hear first?"

"I'll start with the good news."

Toni flipped through the papers and looked over at Skye. "Your husband has appointed you as his POA."

Skye looked confused. "POA? What does that mean?"

"A Power of Attorney which is authorization to represent or act on your husband's behalf in regards to handling his bank accounts, private affairs, business, healthcare, real estate etc, in the event that he should become disabled or legally incapacitated."

"So, who is his Power of Attorney now?"

"For now I am, but of course that's just temporary. Normally a spouse would automatically become a POA, but Sandino has a written and notarized document that says you couldn't become his until you agreed to his terms."

"He's such a fucking asshole," Skye vented. "How much money does he have left anyway?"

Toni looked down at the paperwork she'd recently got from Sandino's accountant. "When you add up Sandino's football pension and all the former endorsement money he had rolled into a separate account over the years, he's still worth a whole lot of money. We're talking about fifteen million."

Skye was speechless for a second. "So, what's the bad news?" she finally asked.

"Well, Sandino also has some restrictions on this document which are, in order for you to become POA, you can never divorce him and you must live in the same residence," Toni continued to read off the paper. "If he is injured or hospitalized you must take care of him at home, no hospitals."

Skye immediately got upset. "What? Do I look like a damn nurse?"

"Skye, please calm down. We'll provide a live-in nurse from his rehab center to help you with his care. I have to inform you though, it's also stated in bold letters if you refuse to follow his demands, you get nothing. However, your kids will get a portion of their trust when they turn twenty-one and the other half at age twenty-five. Sandino stated that, by this time his sons should've established their own successful careers like he always tried to instill in them, and that his money shouldn't be their only source of income."

Skye went ballistic and started ranting and raving.

"I should be entitled to half, regardless after all the shit that crazy muthafucka put me through!"

"Again, Skye please calm down," Toni advised.

When Skye finally calmed down, Toni looked inside the file again and pushed a document across the desk in her direction. Skye looked at the bold letters across the top that read, **Postnuptial Agreement**. Skye's eyes widened, she then dropped her head. She immediately remembered signing a piece of paper that Sandino refused to let her read about two years ago. She'd forgotten all about it.

"That Postnuptial Agreement states that if you ever divorce Sandino you won't be entitled to anything," Toni stated.

Suddenly, the music from Skye's cell phone interrupted them. She continued to shake her head as she dug into her purse to retrieve it. She already knew it was Cruze by the Cee-Lo Green ringtone, *Fool For You*. After missing the call, a text message came shortly afterwards.

Are u ok, he texted.

Skye quickly texted back. ***Hell no, I'll explain later***.

Toni sat somewhat irritated watching Skye as she typed. As soon as Skye placed her phone down on the edge of the desk, she decided to continue.

"Listen Skye, you really need to think about this divorce," Toni said, sliding the divorce papers back in Skye's direction. "Think about how much money you're giving up. Most likely Sandino will never walk again or be able to handle his own affairs. My advice to you honey is to move back home and take care of your husband, so you can get the money you and your family deserve. Not to mention, some woman claiming to be his sister has been frequently calling my office asking about his finances."

Skye's eyebrows crinkled. "Sister? Sandino doesn't have a sister. It's probably one of his many bitches or his crazy ass, money hungry aunt."

"Well, that just goes to show, if you don't take care of him, one of his estranged family members will and then they'll get all his money."

"I don't know," Skye said, shaking her head.

"Listen, you don't have to decide right now. I'll give you a few days to think over the proposal. But I do have to inform you that I have one last bit of bad news."

"And what's that?"

"Sandino has been petitioned for child support."

Once again Skye was stunned. "Child support…from who?"

"I can't reveal that information until I speak to the mother regarding DNA, and the results. Apparently this woman has already taken the test along with the alleged child, so now the court is just waiting on Sandino to take the test."

"Are you serious right now? I think I have a right to know. Why are you taking this woman's side when you're Sandino's lawyer and I'm still legally his wife. The least you could do is tell me her fucking name. Why are you trying to hide the bitch?" Skye was beyond pissed now.

"Listen Skye, in my defense I've already done you and your family a favor. Sandino should've taken the test weeks ago, but because of his situation, I've been able to put everything off. I didn't want to put him or your family through anything else right now. Sandino possibly having an illegitimate child with another woman would send the media into an uproar. You all have been through enough."

"All that sounds good right now, but I still would like to know her name!" Skye continued to belt.

"I can tell you're a little upset so I'm going to end this meeting."

"A *little* upset wouldn't be the correct term," Skye said though teary eyes.

She stood up and snatched the divorce papers off of the desk before throwing her outdated purse over her shoulder and walking out. Everything seemed to move in slow motion as she walked towards the elevator.

I guess Sandino meant what he said…til death do us part, she thought.

Skye walked onto the elevator thinking how crazy life was. Luckily, no one else was on the elevator with her because as soon as the doors closed, she tilted her head back and screamed to the top of her lungs like a mad woman.

"Why the fuck does shit keep happening to me? After all the years of abuse I suffered at the hands of that man. I can't even bare to look him, yet alone take care of his ass!" she shouted.

Skye debated whether or not she should tell Cruze what the meeting was really about. She knew it was important to him that she got a divorce and moved on, but the stakes were a little different now. Skye also knew with that type of money, she and the kids would be set for life. So, until she had time to think things over, she would just have to make up something for now. Skye just hoped Cruze would continue to stand by her side if she decided to take care of Sandino.

When Skye reached the lobby she didn't see Cruze anywhere. She went in her purse to retrieve her phone and call him, but quickly realized that she'd left it upstairs. After her outburst the last thing Skye wanted was to go back inside Toni's office, but she needed her phone. Turning around, she waited for the elevator behind a group of people in the crowded lobby. She then suddenly became annoyed as she listened to a screaming baby in a stroller with a woman several feet in front of the crowd.

"Damn, I wish she would feed that baby or something," Skye said to herself.

When the elevator doors finally opened, surprisingly Toni walked off.

"I'm glad I caught you, Skye. I'm sorry if I upset you, but I was just doing my job," Toni said, passing Skye her phone.

"It is what it is," Skye replied still pissed off.

Toni gave her a nonchalant look before walking back toward the elevator. Skye turned around to leave herself, but paused when she heard a woman say, "Hey, Ms. Vaughn, I was just on my way up to see you for our two o'clock appointment."

When Skye thought she recognized the voice, she abruptly turned around. Her eyes widened while her heart rate began to enhance. It was Asia!

Without a second thought, Skye walked up to Asia and stood in front of her like they were about to go toe to toe at a boxing match. "What the fuck are you doing here?" she fumed.

Asia reached down, grabbed a pacifier and stuck it into the baby's mouth to quiet the screaming down. Skye stared at the baby in the stroller long and hard then placed her angry eyes back on her former friend.

Asia slung her hair from side to side, ignoring Skye's question and evil stare. She wasn't at all dressed appropriately for a business meeting wearing a pair of black sequined leggings and a short pink t-shirt that barely covered her plump ass. Her once flat stomach was now replaced with a huge baby pooch from her obvious pregnancy.

Toni turned and gave Skye eye contact as if she wanted to say something but didn't.

Instead of responding, Asia just held a smirk on her face.

"Bitch, are you just gonna stand there like nothing happened?" Skye roared.

"Skye, I didn't come here to fight. I came to find out how much money my son will be getting from his father," Asia responded.

"I know you didn't say what the fuck I think you said." Skye now knew that Asia was probably the one calling Toni pretending to be Sandino's sister.

"I don't know why you're tripping Skye, it's not like

29

Sandino doesn't have more than enough money to go around."

At that moment, Skye went crazy. She leaped over and grabbed a wad of Asia's hair, then slung her onto the floor, diving on top of her body. Seconds later, she started throwing several jabs, with each one landing on Asia's face. The people standing near the elevator ran over and stood there staring at them like it was a scene from *The Bad Girl's Club*. All Asia could do to defend herself was to hold her head down and scream for help as Skye went ballistic.

"I trusted you bitch!" Skye screamed as she continued to throw several punches.

"Skye, please stop! She has a small child!" Toni pleaded.

People in the lobby stood around watching and pointing as Skye put an old fashion beat down on Asia. A few seconds later, two security officers finally came over and pulled the two women apart. One of the officers helped Asia up off the floor while the other security guard stood in front of Skye.

"Miss, we aren't tolerating this. We've already radioed in for the police," one of the security officers said to Skye.

Toni stopped him. "No, that won't be necessary. She was just about to leave."

The security guard looked at Toni. "We can't have this type of violence in this building, Ms. Vaughn," he said.

Asia went wild when she saw blood on her clothes and strands of long, natural hair on the floor. At no time did she even bother to go check on her screaming baby, who was now being attended to by one of the bystanders. The stroller had been pushed several feet away during the fight. All Asia did was hold her eye which was swelling shut. Skye on the other hand came out of the scuffle with only a few scratches.

At that moment Cruze walked up. "Yo', what's going on?' he asked running over and grabbing Skye from the security officer's hold. "What happened, baby?"

"Asia was fucking Sandino and that's his so-called

baby, that's what's going on!" Skye yelled pointing in the direction of the stroller.

Cruze turned and looked at Asia. He hadn't even recognized her.

"I want that woman arrested for assault!" Asia yelled to the security officer.

Skye lost it. "Sue me bitch, or better yet just take it out of the money you stole from me and my kids. You or that lil' bastard baby will never get a dime of Sandino's money as long as I'm in charge!"

Cruze wondered what Skye meant by that comment as he grabbed her arm. "Come on, let's go. She's not worth it," he said, escorting Skye out the front door.

Once Skye was outside, she paced back and forth like a mad women while Cruze searched for a cab.

"That fucking bastard!" Skye's breathing had become so heavy. "Out of all the woman he cheated on me with, he had to get that bitch pregnant. I should've seen the fucking signs. The way both of them claimed they hated each other so bad. All that shit was a front. That's okay though, I got something for both of those muthafuckas!" she belted.

Cruze shook his head in disbelief as he stood silent. His premonition about Skye not being ready to come back to Miami and the trip becoming a disaster had been confirmed. "Skye, don't beat yourself over it," Cruze said, wrapping his arms around her.

Skye pushed him away. "I'm ready to go home," she replied, walking a few feet away from him.

When Cruze noticed a cab coming he whistled and signed for it to pull up in his direction. He yelled over at Skye and told her to come on. Once inside, he told the driver to take them to their hotel near Bayside.

"I don't feel like staying here, let's go to the airport. We might be able to switch our tickets and get a flight tonight," Skye demanded.

31

"Why are you letting that bitch upset you like this? You knew from day one Asia wasn't shit. Hell, it might not even be Sandino's baby knowing her. You know the bitch is a liar."

Skye didn't say anything for a minute. "So, did you know Sandino was fucking Asia?' she asked with an attitude.

Cruze looked her. "If I did would it make a difference?"

"You're avoiding the question so that must mean you knew. Did you fuck her, too?"

He felt himself getting angry. "Skye, no I've never fucked Asia. I could have if I wanted to, but she wasn't my style. I knew that bitch was poison the very first time I met her."

"Well, I wish you would've told me. Maybe you could've saved me a headache. I hate that no good bitch."

At that moment Cruze looked down at Skye's purse on the seat and saw the divorce papers still inside, which instantly made him infuriated. "So, are you even gonna tell me what the meeting was about? I see you still have the papers."

Skye was nervous to tell Cruze the truth at the moment, so she decided to become defensive in order to take some of the focus off of the truth. She just hoped he would continue to stand by her side no matter what. She paused before speaking,

"Why are you pressuring me? Can I at least have some time to gather my damn thoughts?" she shot back at him.

Cruze didn't respond, he knew Skye had gone through a lot in one day so an argument between them might've just sent her over the edge. Skye was unsure on what to do. Part of her definitely wanted to be in charge of Sandino's money while the other part of her didn't want that life again. Even though she'd already walked away from everything and vowed to never look back, the thought was tempting.

Feeling a headache coming on, Skye rubbed her temples for a few minutes then reached in her purse and took one of her pills. As Cruze looked at her and shook his head, Skye laid her head back on the seat. She desperately wished she could find Ms. Petra. A person who she could always confide in and someone she truly trusted. Skye didn't like keeping secrets from Cruze, but needed a little time to let the ultimatum soak in her mind.

Meanwhile, Cruze looked out of the window wondering if Skye had a good reason for not giving the lawyer the divorce papers as she promised. As soon as she calmed down, he planned to get to the bottom of it. He didn't like the idea that she was keeping something from him. But then again, he was doing the same thing. He prayed Skye wouldn't leave him if she found out he was back in the streets.

The rest of the cab ride was silent.

LIFE *After* A BALLA

Chapter Four

Asia drove down the street furious after leaving the meeting with the Sandino's lawyer. *Not only did I get beat up by Skye, but that lawyer was on some bullshit,* she thought.

After all the commotion had calmed down and they got upstairs in her office, Asia immediately started asking personal questions about Sandino's money. Toni became irritated and told Asia that she couldn't talk about her client's finances just as she'd informed her numerous times over the phone. Toni went on to say that the only reason she'd agreed to meet with Asia was because she was tired of the constant calls to her office. She then told Asia that things were getting complicated and from that point on, she only wanted to talk to Asia's lawyer. When Asia told her she didn't have a lawyer, Toni suggested that she get one, then ended the meeting. Asia wondered if Skye had something to do with Toni not wanting to give her any information.

"Those bitches are probably in cahoots trying to keep me from getting any of Sandino's money," she said to herself. "And why the fuck is it taking so long for Sandino to take that DNA test!"

Asia didn't know what was going on, but she was in desperate need of some money… bad. In fact, that's the only reason she'd kept the baby in the first place. A child by Sandino meant a nice payday.

"That bitch Skye better not try to interfere with my loot. She's just upset that I fucked her husband and got the golden ticket in my back seat," Asia said, glancing over her shoulder at her one month old son's car seat. A son she'd named Sandino Lamar Washington Jr.

Either way, Asia knew she'd out smarted Skye once before and could do it again if she had to, especially since the matter involved money. She was the queen of conning and stealing, it was the only way she knew how to survive.

When she turned onto 21st Street, two blocks from Collins Avenue, Asia looked around at the scenery. It was always so lively in the South Beach neighborhood. This was her favorite spot to be in Miami because the area offered everything for anybody. There were tons of trendy restaurants, one-of-a-kind boutiques, and at night it transformed into the best nightlife ever. She laughed while counting the number of times the same dudes in a hot ass Ferrari drove past her, not going anywhere just cruising around trying to pick up women. She absolutely loved Miami and was so glad to be out of cold ass Chicago.

When she first arrived, Asia took some of the money she'd stolen from Skye and rented an expensive condo overlooking Lake Michigan. The place was absolutely fabulous with over 1,600 square feet along with cathedral ceilings, bamboo hard wood floors, and a beautiful kitchen with top of the line appliances. Things were going great and she was starting to experience the essence of the Windy City.

While eating at Michael Jordan's steakhouse on Michigan Avenue one night, Asia befriended a nicely dressed woman at the bar who just so happened to be the wife of a Chicago Bulls player. Asia had once again hit the jackpot and within a few weeks managed to ease her way amongst the rich and famous. After hanging out in the sky box at every Chicago Bulls

Jackie D.

home game, Asia was on her way to snagging her own NBA player until she started getting sick and later found out she nine weeks pregnant. In fact that sickness became a part of her everyday life until she was well into her second trimester. But in typical Asia style, finding out she was going to be a mother still didn't stop her from trying to find a man. She was constantly out clubbing and even had a couple of drinks. But with a growing belly and no matter how hard she turned on her sexy charm, no one seemed interested.

Asia's plans to save her cash and quickly find a balla with money to take care of her quickly went out the window. She spent her entire pregnancy lonely and depressed. She even had to drive herself to the hospital when she went into labor and had the baby all alone. The only thing that kept her going was the fact that she knew she would be set for life. After doing the calculations, Asia knew it was definitely Sandino's baby, which was certainly gonna be her meal ticket. Even though she was well aware of the shooting and all that he'd gone through, Asia still planned to take Sandino for every dime she could.

After her trip down memory lane, a cold chill suddenly ran over her when she glanced across at the street and saw The Bay View Plaza condo's where Keon used to live. Asia remembered the day their romance turned sour and he tried to kill her. The vision of his body laying there with a bullet in his forehead from her .32 caliber handgun was still etched in her head.

I hate the fact that I killed Keon, but he tried to kill me first, so I had to do what I had to do, she thought. *And I would do that shit all over again if the situation was the same.*

She felt lucky that nothing had ever come out of the Keon situation like a first degree murder charge. When Asia finally pulled up to the Seagull Hotel, reality hit her in face. Even though it was only $87.00 a night, she was still low on cash and didn't know how much longer she could afford to stay there.

Her mind raced thinking about how she could get some money to hold her over until the paternity tests came back. After getting rid of her old phone, she didn't know how to get in touch with any of her old men. She needed to go out to the club and let the nigga's know she was back in town, but she also knew that wasn't going to work either since she didn't have a babysitter.

"Shit, think Asia," she said out loud. Getting frustrated, she came up with the best option. "I'm about to pay Sandino's ass a visit. Maybe once he gets a look at his son, he can tell that bitch of a lawyer to write me a damn check," she said, grabbing her white Evo cell phone off the charger.

She went to the internet icon and typed in the name Sandino Washington hoping to find out where he was. With all the media attention since his shooting, reporters and even bloggers seemed to be tracking his every move. Asia waited for several results to come up. A few of them were about his old football injuries, so she kept searching until finally seeing a recent article talking about his status along with the name of the rehabilitation facility. After putting in the address in her GPS system, Asia displayed a huge smile.

"On a mission to get my money," she said, turning up the music when she heard *Niggas in Paris* by Kanye and Jay-Z playing on the radio.

Twenty minutes later, Asia arrived at the facility. She pulled out her foundation and makeup brush before applying a heavy coat on her face trying to cover up the huge red mark under her left eye. After checking her appearance one last time, Asia got out of the truck and opened the back door to take her son out. She frowned at the strong smell of urine and realized she hadn't changed him all day. Letting out a huge

Jackie D.

sigh, she pulled him out of the seat, then proceeded to change his soiled pamper. Asia was irritated. She didn't realize how much work it took to be a mother, and had to admit that she wasn't looking forward to eighteen years of being responsible for someone other than herself. When Asia finished changing the diaper, she placed the baby back in his car seat and headed towards the facility.

Out of nowhere several reporters and photographers ran up surrounding Asia like a pack of wolves then started snapping her picture and asking questions.

"Are you here to see Sandino Washington? Can you give us an update on his progress?" one reporter asked, passing her a business card.

"Are you family? Whose baby is this?" another reported blurted out snapping pictures of her son. With microphones pushed in her face and the constant flashes of cameras Asia felt trapped and violated.

"No, I'm not here to see Sandino Washington, now move out my way so I can get inside," she demanded pushing her way past the mob of vultures.

The paparazzi and news reporters walked away disappointed that they weren't getting a juicy story to report. Once inside, Asia cleared her throat to get the chubby nurse's attention once she reached the front desk.

"Hello, may I help you?" the nurse asked.

"Yes, I'm here to see my husband, Sandino Washington," Asia responded.

The nurse looked at her funny. "What's your name? Are you a reporter?"

"No, not at all. My name is Skye. Skye Washington," Asia answered.

The nurse's expression finally changed. "Oh, it's nice to finally meet you, Mrs. Washington. Everyone has been wondering when you were finally going to come visit him." The nurse studied her again. "You look so different from all the

39

photos they show on T.V."

"Yeah, I changed my hair and added a few pounds," Asia said trying to play it off.

"I can understand that. I've put on a few myself," the nurse said, patting her stomach.

Bitch, stop lying. You've added way more than a few. A ton is more like it," Asia thought.

"And look at that beautiful baby." When the nurse noticed the baby's blue dinosaur onesie she said, "I thought Mr. Washington had two sons and a one year old daughter."

Asia was becoming very irritated with the nosey nurse. "He does...I mean we do. This is my nephew. I'm just watching him for my brother for a little while. Can I please see my husband now?"

"Oh, yes of course."

"So, what room is he in?" Asia asked.

"Please don't be offended Mrs. Washington, but do you have your ID? We're supposed to ask when it concerns your husband. You know since he's a high profile patient."

Asia had to think of something quick. "Actually, I don't. I was in such a rush on my way here, and left it in the hotel. It's been a long day with me dealing with my nephew." She gave the nurse a sad look. "I can go back and get it. It may take me a while since my hotel is across town, but it's fine." When Asia displayed an exhausted expression, and turned around the nurse grabbed her arm.

"Don't worry about it, Mrs. Washington." She looked around then lowered her voice. "I'm sure you're dying to see your husband, so I'll make an exception this time. Come this way I'll show you to his room."

Asia thanked her before giving the nurse a fake smile and following her down the hall. She looked around at all the patients in the hallway and instantly became sick on her stomach. She hated hospitals, but was in desperate need for Sandino to meet his son. When they entered the room, Asia was shocked to see that the once big and muscular Sandino was now much smaller. It looked like he'd lost at least sixty pounds or more. He sat in a wheelchair near the window asleep.

"Mr. Washington, your wife is finally here to see you," the nurse announced.

At that moment, Sandino's eyes opened wide as if he was excited by her words. However, when he saw Asia standing there, a frown suddenly appeared on his face.

"I'll leave you two alone," the nurse said, walking towards the door.

Asia couldn't help but stare at the side of Sandino's head that looked as if an entire section had been removed. "Why does his head look like that?"

"That's from the surgery where doctor's had to remove part of his skull to retrieve the bullet fragments," the nurse advised.

"Damn," Asia said under her breath. "Can he talk?"

Sandino was slumped over with dried up saliva on the side of his mouth and crust between his eyes. The oversized sweat suit he wore swallowed his now slimmer physique and his large feet were turned together in an awkward position between the petal guards of his wheelchair. It shocked Asia to see him that way.

"He's working on it. He can mumble a few things, but nothing comes out that well other than yes and no sometimes."

Asia looked at her but didn't respond. She wasn't used to Sandino not being the asshole he once was.

"Let me know if you need anything."

When the nurse left the room, Asia walked over and sat in a chair near Sandino staring at the large scar that stretched across his head. Sandino watched her as well.

"Long time no see, Sandino. Damn, you all fucked up," she said, staring at him once again. "I just wanted to come by and introduce you to your son." Asia took the baby out of the car seat and placed him close to Sandino's face. "Doesn't he look just like you? I named him Sandino Jr. Thinking about calling him SJ for short."

Sandino cut his eyes at the baby. He studied him for along time before directing his eyes back on Asia.

"I just came here to tell you that I need money. I know Skye and your lawyer are trying to block your third son outta his share and I think that's fucked up. I know you're probably still mad at me about that money I stole, but that shit was in the past. What's important now is making sure your son is taken care of. I know you believe in making sure your kids always have the best," she said.

Sandino's eyes turned angry. He moved his mouth trying to speak and after stuttering for a few seconds he yelled out the word no, then spit on Asia. Luckily, the saliva didn't land anywhere near her face.

She jumped up with the baby in her arms. "I know you didn't just spit on me you handicapped muthafucka!" She stared at him for a few seconds, before returning the glob of spit. She then reached for her cell phone and snapped several pictures of him.

"I tried to be nice to your evil ass by coming here like a lady to ask for your help. But since you want to disrespect me, I'm about to disrespect you. I'm sure all the paparazzi outside would give me big money for these pictures of your sickly looking ass. Not to mention I could see the headlines now, ex pro ball player Sandino's Washington's illegitimate son. One way or the other… you will pay!" Asia yelled. She quickly placed the baby back inside the car seat as the nurse walked back into the room.

"Is everything alright in here, Mrs. Washington?"

"Don't call me that shit. I'm not Mrs. Washington. It's no way could I ever be married to this selfish ass bastard!"

As soon as the nurse's eyes widened, Asia ran out the room and headed back to her truck. After securing the baby's seat back into the base, it didn't take long for her to start up the engine and skid out of the parking lot.

"What have I gotten myself into?" she asked out loud.

Asia didn't like kids and definitely wasn't feeling the whole mommy thing, so something had to be done. She couldn't take care of a baby broke. She needed a nanny and a nice house on the beach like Skye once had.

"I'll hold onto these pictures of Sandino as back up reassurance. I won't have a problem making a few calls and selling them to the tabloids to get some cash if it comes down to that," Asia said, trying to come up with a plan. She got upset when the baby started crying.

"Shut up, I need to think!"

Jackie D.

Chapter Five

When Skye and Cruze pulled up in front of her apartment complex on Sweetwater Road late the next evening, the cloudy and dull Georgia skies had her missing Miami's beautiful weather already. Georgia was a far cry from sunny Florida. Although her new neighborhood was far better than the one in Marietta, where she often witnessed drug transactions and young boys rolling dice on the curb, it still wasn't the type of environment she wanted to raise her kids in. Not to mention, she was tired of apartment living.

When Cruze pulled up in front of the building to let her out, Skye looked over at him with an evil expression. Tired and worn out, she was still pissed at him for causing them to miss their early morning eight a.m. flight. Instead of traveling for only an hour and fifty minutes, that time had been turned into ten hours after Cruze heavily insisted that they drive back to Georgia versus being on standby for the next flight. Skye didn't understand his logic, so not only did she refuse to help drive back, but she also refused to answer his questions about the meeting. Each time he asked, her response was always the same. "I don't feel like discussing it." With Cruze eventually getting an attitude, the two of them didn't talk much. It was obvious that they both had a lot on their mind.

When Skye gathered her things and opened the car door to get out, Cruze grabbed her arm. "Where my kiss at?"

She looked at him funny. "Are you serious? You've been acting salty the entire trip and now you want a kiss."

"I'm not salty. I just don't see what the big secret about that meeting is, that's all. But I'll wait for you to tell me in your own time," he replied.

It was the nicest thing he'd said since they left Florida. Skye reached over and planted her lips on his, giving him a quick peck. When she got out of the seat Cruze patted her on the ass.

"Just be naked and ready for me when I get back," he said with a huge smile.

"Just don't' be all night," Skye responded. "You're just going to the airport to take the rental car back and get your car, right?"

"You obviously weren't listening to me while we were driving. Remember, I told you that the dealership just got in a new shipment of cars today. One of my co-workers called out sick earlier, so I just need to run down there and help."

"But it's after seven o'clock. The dealership should be closed," Skye replied. She loved the fact the Cruze was such a provider, but she hated his job as a car salesman for some reason.

"It is, so that's why it's a good time for me to go down there and help. Don't worry, baby. I'm not gonna be gone all night."

"Okay," Skye finally gave in before closing the door.

Cruze rolled down the window before pulling off. "Love you!"

"Love you, too!" Skye responded.

Needing to figure out what to do about the whole Sandino situation anyway, it was probably best that Cruze was leaving. Him harboring over her wasn't what she needed right now

As soon as she started walking towards her apartment, some young boys in a nearby car began to whistle and holler at her.

"Damn, you look good shawty, can I get with you?" one of them yelled.

Skye ignored them and kept walking. She shook her head thinking, *I hate disrespectful ass children. I can't wait to get inside and pour myself a glass of Moscato so I can relax and block everything out.*

As Skye walked closer to her apartment, she was surprised when she saw Lydia and Payton headed in her direction. Payton who had just learned to walk, waddled over with a big smile spread across her small face.

"Ma Ma!" Payton called out.

"Hey, baby girl," Skye said, picking her daughter up and kissing her fat, juicy cheeks. She then directed her attention to Lydia. "What the world are you doing here? How did you find out where we lived? Where's Kareem?" Skye questioned her.

She hadn't seen her old neighbor since they'd moved forty-five minutes away, eight months ago. Ever since the shooting, Skye really didn't trust anybody around her family and she certainly didn't want to answer any questions about Sandino.

"Kareem called and asked if I could pick up Payton because he had something to do and you were out of town. Is something wrong?" Lydia asked.

"No, it's just that Kareem was supposed to be watching her, that's all." Skye wondered what Kareem had to do that was so important. She also tried to keep her cool in order not to offend her former babysitter. "I can't believe you drove all the way out here."

"Well, when Kareem called, I jumped at the opportunity to see my little princess. It's been so long," Lydia said, poking Payton in her stomach. Payton grinned and put her hands over her eyes acting bashful. "You know I never mind babysitting Payton. She's always been such a good baby. I miss you all so much. It doesn't feel the same without you being my neighbor anymore."

"We miss you too, but I had to get away from all that madness, we needed a fresh start."

"I can understand that, by the way, how is Jordan doing in Spanish 2 this year?" Lydia asked.

"Well, school just started last month, but he's doing well so far, and I owe that all to you," Skye proudly stated, giving her a hug.

"No problem. I loved tutoring Jordan, he's a smart boy and loves to learn." Lydia looked at her watch. "I was just about to take Payton to Chucky Cheese for a little while if that's okay with you. I want to spend a little time with her."

Skye was a little hesitant, but decided that she probably would've been overreacting if she told Lydia that wasn't a good idea. "No, of course I don't mind, she loves that place," Skye said, kissing Payton once more before putting her down.

"I won't have her out too long. We should be back by 8:30," Lydia replied, grabbing Payton by the hand.

"That's fine. Bye my sweetie pie," Skye said, waving.

Payton waved her little hand backwards.
"Bye...bye...bye."

Skye loved her daughter, but the extended break from the one year old little terror was appreciated. Ever since she'd started walking, Payton got into everything and had been wearing everybody out. The only person she had wrapped around her little finger was Cruze. Payton could do no wrong in his eyes.

Lydia suddenly turned around. "Oh yeah, before I forget. There was some man knocking on your old apartment door not too long after you moved. He then started walking around the neighborhood asking questions."

Skye stood wondering who it could've possibly been.

Then again there were so many reporters coming up to her door after the incident, it could've been anyone.

"See, this is one of the main reasons why I moved. Did he say who he was? Skye asked. "Was he from some news station?"

"I don't think so, and when I asked him his name he didn't answer. He just asked if I knew where you moved and I told him no. Even if I had known where you all were moving I would've never given him the information."

Skye shook her head. "I know, and I thank you for that."

"I tried to call and tell you, but you never answered any of my calls."

"I'm sorry, Lydia. It's just that after all that happened, I kinda went into a little funk. I really didn't want to talk to anybody."

"Don't worry. I understand."

"If you see him again, let me know though."

"Will do, he was really cute, too," Lydia joked.

After saying goodbye one last time, Skye finally headed inside wondering who the mystery man was. *Another thing to add to my worries*, she thought.

She entered her apartment and dropped her keys and purse on the console table in her small foyer. When she heard the T.V. in the living room playing really loud she instantly became irritated. It was a never ending battle with her sons when it came to leaving the T.V. on whenever they weren't watching it. Skye knew it was a hard habit for them to break since they'd grown up with Ms. Petra always doing everything for them. At that moment, she wondered again what Kareem had to do that was so important.

"It's not like his lazy ass has a job," she said to herself.

Deciding to deal with him later, Skye kicked off her shoes and glanced at *The Wendy Williams* show and caught herself saying, "How you doin'?"

Turning the volume down a bit, she walked to her bedroom to throw on a pair of leggings along with a big t-shirt to get comfortable. She'd been in the same tight jeans for ten long hours. However, when Skye turned the corner her eyes almost popped out of her head when she saw Kareem sitting on her bed with his head tilted back and a female down on his knees giving him head. She immediately became enraged.

"What the fuck? Have you lost your damn mind, Kareem?" she yelled.

The woman turned around, wiped her mouth and stood up looking at Skye with a smirk. Kareem quickly pulled his pants up and tried to apologize.

"Oh shit...my bad, Ma. Things got a little hot and heavy and we couldn't make it to my room."

"What? Hot and heavy my ass, get the hell out of my damn room. Is this what you had to do that was so important? Who the hell is this woman?" Skye pointed. "You know I don't want any strangers in my house!"

"Ma, calm down. This is Le Le. She's not a stranger," Kareem replied.

"So, this is your mother," Le Le said with a long stare.

"And you're the infamous Le Le," Skye replied while looking the woman up and down.

Le Le's long, jet black weave was all over the place from Kareem rubbing his hands threw it. She took her fingers and attempted to try and comb it out of her face. After hearing Kareem talk about her for the past few weeks, Skye was shocked to see how old the woman seemed to be. With a name like Le Le, Skye thought she was Kareem's age. However, she couldn't hate on the woman's skin, which was absolutely flawless.

"You should've had more class about yourself. Having sex in my bedroom is tacky and a little juvenile don't you think?" Skye said to her.

"Look, I'm sorry, but your son was the one who invited

me over here. How the hell was I supposed to know it was your room? You better fall the fuck back," she shot back with an attitude.

"Who the fuck are you telling to fall back?" Skye asked walking up on her. "Bitch, you're in *my* house!"

Kareem walked over and stood in front of the woman. "Ma, chill out."

"Kareem, let's go before this shit gets out of hand!" Le Le stated with authority, then walked towards the door.

"Kareem, you're not going anywhere. Now, this bossy bitch can get the fuck out, but you're not leaving!" Skye yelled. She looked at Le Le. "Did you know he was only seventeen?"

Kareem quickly stepped in before things got escalated. "Ma, why you trippin? How you gonna tell me how to live my life or who I should be with when you keep switching up men. You got yet another man living up in here. I like Cruze and all, but you got this nigga up in here acting like he run shit now. You so weak, you can't even be alone without a man telling you what to do. Now you trying to judge Le Le and you don't even know her."

Le Le put her hand on hip and smiled. She was impressed that Kareem was standing up for her.

"I don't want to know her," Skye responded.

Le Le frowned. "And I don't want to know you either!"

"Now you see why I don't tell you nothing that's going on in my life cause you so negative," Kareem continued.

"Don't try and flip this shit on me," Skye replied. "I know a conniving bitch when I see one. And she has the nerve to be disrespectful!"

"I'm not gonna be too many more bitches," Le Le fired back.

All of a sudden, Kareem's bad temper quickly emerged as he picked up a lamp and threw it across the room.

Skye's eyes lit up once again. "Kareem, are you crazy?

Throw something else and see what the fuck happens. Don't let me embarrass you in front of this broad. Just because your ass has a little mustache now doesn't make you grown."

Le Le who was obviously startled by Kareem's behavior picked up her purse and headed out of the room. "I'll be in the car Kareem, so don't keep me waiting. We can pick up where we left off at my place," she said, giving Skye an evil look.

"I'm right behind you," Kareem responded.

Moments later, Le Le made her way toward the front door. As soon as Kareem heard the door close, he directed his attention right back to his mother.

"I can't believe you just disrespected me in front of that lady. How old is she anyway?" Skye questioned.

"What difference does it make? Why don't you go pop one of those pills and chill out. I love Le Le and she's not going anywhere so you might as well learn to like her."

"Love? How the hell can you love somebody you just fucking met? How long have you known her? About three…maybe four weeks? I thought you were seeing some young girl, not some old ass cougar."

"You need to stop talking about my girl like that. Do you see me around here talking about your *third* man that way? Where is he anyway? Any other time he's right up under you," Kareem shot back.

All Skye could think about was the fact that she was so tired of being disrespected. The more Kareem continued to argue back, the madder she became. "I'm sick of your damn mouth, Kareem!" Rage consumed her and she hauled off and slapped him as hard as she could.

He stepped back absolutely shocked holding his face. As much as it hurt Skye to strike him, a good slap across the face was the only way she could get her point across that she would no longer tolerate his lack of respect.

A few seconds later, Kareem formed a fist. "I advise

you not to do that again or…" he tried to threaten.

Skye's jaws tightened as she walked up in her son's face ready for a battle. "Or what? I wish you would hit me. You know what, you act just like your damn…" Skye paused. They hadn't mentioned Sandino's name since the night he was shot.

"Go ahead, say it, just like my father? I'll never be like him and I'll never marry a weak ass woman like you either!" he yelled, slamming the door.

LIFE *After* A BALLA

Chapter Six

Forty minutes later, Kareem and Le Le entered her five bedroom home in Dunwoody. While she put her purse down and kicked off her shoes to get comfortable, Kareem was in his own little world still mad about the fight with his mother.

"I can't believe she disrespected you like that," he said, pacing back and forth.

Deciding not to respond, Le Le went into the kitchen and poured him a shot of peach Ciroc to calm his nerves. When she returned to the living room, he was still pacing the floor talking to himself.

"Here you go baby, maybe this will calm you down."

Kareem took the glass out of her hand and immediately turned it up taking it to the head. He then slammed the glass down on the table and continued to mumble under his breath.

"She doesn't want me to start talking about that murder."

Le Le's body instantly stiffened, and her eyes narrowed. "What did you just say? A murder?"

Suddenly, Kareem snapped out of it and looked over at her realizing he was talking too much. "What? Why you all up in my mouth? I didn't say shit about no murder."

Le Le looked at him funny. She didn't like his tone and

Jackie D.

she knew what she'd heard "Yes, the hell you did."

Kareem tried his best to play it off. "You tripping."

"Look, I'm too old to be dealing with some dumb shit. If you're some type of drug dealer or gang banger, then you need to roll. I can take your ass back right now."

"I didn't say shit about no murder!" Kareem reiterated. As he continued to pace, Le Le decided to let it go for now and sat down on the couch. "My mother needs to let me live my life. She's always so hard on me, but treats my damn brother like a king. I guess she thinks he's gonna be a pro balla or something," Kareem said, sitting down beside her. He propped his feet up on her leather ottoman and threw his head back.

Le Le knew the argument had him pissed and she'd never seen him so upset before. But she was also glad he'd finally put his controlling mother in her place. She was sick of Skye always calling Kareem every hour on the hour asking where he was like he was a child. So when Skye walked in on them having oral sex in her bedroom, Le Le got a bit of enjoyment out of seeing her upset. Besides, she hated momma's boys.

Le Le watched as Kareem sat with a somber look on his face looking off into space. She was at lost for words because she'd never seen this side of him and didn't want to say the wrong thing. In his daze, Kareem wondered what was really going on with his mother. The way she'd flipped out on him just didn't make sense. He knew her well enough to know something else was bothering her. However, he also knew that she'd never steered him wrong when it came to advice either.

"I wanna apologize for putting you through that. My mother thinks anybody who comes around that she doesn't know is either shady or wants something from us."

"Well, after learning who your father is I can't say that I blame her for that. It's some crazy people out here," she replied.

"Yeah, but that obviously doesn't stop her from getting

56

Jackie D.

a new boyfriend. I hate that she always gotta have a nigga up in her bed."

"Damn, you make it seem like she's had a thousand of them. How many was it before Cruze," Le Le continued to pry.

"Just one."

"Oh really. How long did he last?" she questioned.

Kareem paused for a second. "Man, I don't wanna talk about my mother anymore." He looked over at his girl. "What I wanna know is why are you with me, Le Le? I mean you definitely got your shit together. Look at how you dress and the way you live. I can't buy you shit like this. You could have any man you want. Like a man your own age." He glanced around the room, secretly wondering how she could afford such a nice house by herself.

"I guess it was just fate, Kareem. When we met that day at Perimeter Mall and we started talking, I felt an instant connection with you. That has never happened to me before. And once we started spending time together, I really started feeling you. To me, age ain't nothing but a number, baby. All I know is your mother might as well get over it because I'm not going anywhere."

"Yeah, we did hit it off. Talking to you that day was like talking to an old friend instead of a stranger. The conversation was so good I stayed too long on my break and got fired that day," Kareem said with a smirk.

"You didn't need that bullshit ass job at Chick-fil-A anyway. Don't I give you whatever you need? By the way, I didn't forget that you want those new Jordan's. We can go to the mall and get them tomorrow if you want," Le Le said, blowing him a kiss.

"Okay, thanks baby, you do hold me down," he replied.

"I'm here for you. Feel free to talk to me about anything. I can tell it's a lot going on inside that head of yours. And you told me you've been through a lot. I'll just be glad when you feel comfortable enough to open up more and share

Jackie D.

some of it with me."

Kareem stared at his girl. He had it bad for her. She was a grown woman who knew how to make a man feel good, physically, mentally and financially. He also enjoyed spending time with her, not to mention she was a huge sports fan. She earned major brownie points for that.

"I'll let you in when you let me in," Kareem told her. "I still don't know a lot about you either. Like, what do you do for a living?"

"I don't want to talk about that now. I wanna do this."

Suddenly Le Le stood up then slid her Twisted Heart velour sweat pants down revealing her sexy lace underwear. She placed her hands inside her panties and started fingering herself; then removed one of her hands and licked her fingers while continuing to rub on her clit with the other hand. As Kareem's dick began to throb, Le Le did a little dance while stepping out of her panties reveling a cleanly shaved pussy.

"Let me cheer you up," she said in a sexy voice.

Kareem watched closely as she made her way over toward him. As Le Le removed her t-shirt and rubbed on her nice big breasts, Kareem's dick rose instantly. Even at age thirty-three, Le Le was a very attractive woman with high cheek bones, bronze skin and a deep set of dimples. She definitely could've passed for the actress Gabrielle Union. Her body was perfectly toned and flawless. She didn't look at all her age and Kareem wondered how his mother could tell she was that much older than him.

Le Le dropped down to her knees and unbuttoned Kareem's jeans. Unable to contain the anticipation, Kareem quickly pulled down his pants along with his boxers.

"Now maybe this time we can finish without any interruptions," she said, putting his dick in her mouth.

Le Le sucked slow and passionate, at first teasing and driving Kareem crazy. When he felt his legs getting weak he quickly tried to think of something else to keep from cumming as she put her skills to work and forcefully started sucking and jerking him off at the same time.

"Ooohhh, shit baby, this feels so good," he moaned.

"Say my name," she demanded. When he didn't respond, she got a little more forceful. "Say my damn name!"

"Le Le," he told her. "I want to taste you."

Le Le smirked. She wasn't about to turn that offer down so she stopped sucking, changed positions with him and spread her legs. Kareem went down pushing his head deep into her nest. His face was saturated with her juices as he sucked then nibbled on her clit and stuck his tongue in and out of her pussy. His slurping noises drove her insane. She had no idea how a young man his age could please her like that.

"I want you inside me now," she mumbled.

Following her demands, Kareem lifted his head before climbing on top of her and putting his raw dick into her dripping hot box. He stroked in and out going faster with each thrust.

"You feel good, baby," she moaned.

"Is this is my pussy?" he whispered in her ear.

"Yessss, it's yours, Kareem."

He reached under her butt, grabbing her ass checks, digging even deeper.

"Yes, baby, fuck me harder!" Le Le screamed. She tightened up her walls around his dick when she felt herself about to cum. "I'm cummingggg!" She grabbed onto his young frame as she climaxed and released her juices all over his dick.

"Damn, this shit is good," Kareem added. "I'm cumming, too." His body stiffened as he groaned and unloaded a load of cum inside her.

The two layed out of breath in each other's arms on the couch for awhile until Le Le heard Kareem snoring. She stared at the mole under his lip. It was hard to believe he was so much younger than her. Thinking back to her past relationships, he seemed to be more mature than some of her former lovers. Not to mention he was much better in bed. Youth was definitely a plus when it came to sex. Since Kareem could go all night, she'd finally found a partner that satisfied her appetite for sex.

Le Le eased Kareem's arm off of her and slid her body away without disturbing him. She lightly walked to her bedroom, went inside her huge walk-in closet and retrieved a locked box. She then reached inside the pocket of her mink coat that she hardly wore anymore and pulled out a key. She peeped down the hall making sure Kareem was still asleep in the living room. When the coast was clear, she quietly closed her bedroom door and locked it. She then sat on her black leather, king-sized platform bed, put the key in the box and opened it. Le Le fumbled through the box until she pulled out a picture and immediately kissed it. A tear ran down her face as she started talking to the picture.

"Don't be mad, I'm just having fun with him for now. It won't last long."

Kareem woke up on the couch at Le Le's house an hour later. As soon as he opened his eyes, the argument between him and his mother instantly popped back into his head again. He felt bad that he'd talked to her in such a disrespectful way, but lately the whole situation with her and Cruze was getting to him. He'd been holding how he felt about their relationship in for months, so it seemed like the perfect opportunity to air out his feelings. He needed a break from her and the reminder that his life was so fucked up. Whenever the visions of Justice dying and his father getting shot popped into his head, he would do anything he could to block it out. But seeing Cruze on a regular basis was making it harder to forget.

Jackie D.

But being around Le Le helped him take his mind off all that. She really made him want to do something with his life. Luckily, he'd managed to graduate high school back in June, and even though Kareem decided not to go to college, he still wanted to make something of himself. With him receiving probation for his prior possession charge it was only right that he found a way to somehow make his mother proud even though it seemed as if nothing pleased her these days. He also had to find a way to please Le Le. With a woman like her, Kareem knew she wouldn't want to be with a loser. Feeling the dryness of his throat, he got up and walked to the kitchen to get something to drink; he could still taste Le Le's pussy in his mouth. When he called out her name and she didn't answer he wondered where she was. As soon as he walked into the kitchen, he noticed a note on the granite counter.

Kareem, since you were sleeping so well, I didn't want to wake you. I had to go out for a while. There's a leftover plate of food in the fridge if you get hungry. I hope you're feeling better about the argument with your mother now. Maybe you should stay with me for a while and give her time to cool off. I really enjoy having you here with me. Be back soon.

Le Le

Kareem opened the fridge and pulled out the plate she'd left for him. He then took the foil off stuck it in the microwave and heated it up. He walked to the bathroom wondering where she'd gone.

"She's never left me at her place alone like this before. I hope I didn't scare her away today showing her my crazy side for the first time," he mumbled.

As Kareem stood on the heated marble floors in her bathroom taking a piss, he looked around at her five-star bathroom. It had a basin stone sink and copper rust slate tile in the shower. She definitely had some money because the rest of her home was just as nice. It puzzled Kareem as to why she didn't

61

Jackie D.

have a man before he came along.

How can she afford all this shit, he wondered. *She probably used to mess with some baller. And if she did, how the hell am I gonna compete with that?*

When the microwave beeped letting him know his food was done, Kareem flushed the toilet, washed his hands and headed back to the kitchen. He opened the fridge, grabbed some juice and turned it up leaning against the counter.

"Le Le would probably be pissed off if she saw me drinking from the container like this," he said, laughing to himself.

Seconds later he glanced at the note she'd left him again admiring her penmanship. However, when he reached down to pick it up it fell to the floor on the opposite side. His eye's increased twice their normal size and he stood stiff trying to comprehend what he saw on the back.

"What the hell?"

Chapter Seven

The next morning Skye was awakened by the sound of Payton crying. When she opened her eyes the sun was beaming brightly through the blinds of her bedroom window. After glancing at the clock that read 8:45 a.m. she looked over at the empty spot beside her, and realized that Cruze hadn't come home.

"Oh, hell no. We're not about to start this staying out shit again. I don't care how mad we get with each other," she said, picking up her cell phone and dialing his number.

When it went straight to voicemail, she called back three more times, then decided to leave a message when she heard the beep.

"Cruze, where the hell are you? Why didn't you come home last night? Call me back," Skye said, hanging up.

Feeling pissed and worried all at the same time, Skye jumped up and grabbed Payton out of her crib when she started crying. "Good morning, little girl. Are you hungry?" Skye said, kissing her daughter on her cheek. "Let's go in the kitchen and get you some juice, then I'll fix you something to eat."

Skye wondered why Jordan hadn't come into her room and got Payton like he did every morning as part of his regular ritual. She was so thankful for her son, who was beyond help-ful. When she passed his room a few moments later, her question was answered after seeing him sound asleep with his mouth wide open.

All those late football practices are wearing my poor son out, she thought

Skye then glanced across the hall into Kareem's room and immediately noticed his bed was still made up, which meant he hadn't come home either. She was pissed off even more that he hadn't called to let her know where he was.

"I know that bitch, Le Le, probably influenced him to stay out."

When Skye got closer to the living room and saw a body on the couch with a blanket draped over their head, she breathed a sigh of relief that Cruze had come home after all. He was known for falling asleep after watching movies late at night. Before she could wake him up, Payton started crying again, this time having a full tantrum by kicking her feet and moving her head from side to side.

"Okay little girl, calm down," Skye reacted.

After putting some apple juice in one of Payton's bottles she headed back into the living room to wake Cruze up and drill him about what time he'd come in. However, when she got to the couch and pulled the blanket back, Skye was shocked to see that it was Kareem laying there...not Cruze.

"What are you doing out here or should I ask what time did you come home?" Skye asked with an attitude. She then frowned up her nose. "You smell just like sex. I know you did-n't come in here and lay your nasty ass on my couch!" she yelled.

A sleepy and dazed Kareem looked up and wondered why his mother was bothering him so early in the morning.

"Ma, please don't start with me again. I'm tired," he said, turning over.

Skye decided to leave him alone for now since her main

concern was Cruze, but the shit definitely wasn't over. She headed back to her room to get her cell phone and call him once again. As soon as she laid Payton back down in her crib, Skye wondered what type of lie he would come up with for staying out this time. Was it really work related or was he going to try and pull the same stunt he did the month before saying that he'd gotten drunk with the boys and fell asleep in the car?

I forgave his ass that time, but I'm not gonna keep falling for that shit, Skye thought.

After calling Cruze's phone at least five times and it continuously going straight to voicemail, Skye's head started to spin as she took her fist and pounded it repeatedly on her bed.

She then decided to text him as if that would make a difference.

Cruze, where are you? You need to call me A.S.A.P, WTF? Skye typed, and then hit send.

Why would he take me through this if he knows Sandino used to do the same shit?

Her blood began to boil, as each minute passed and Cruze never text back. After waiting for almost twenty minutes, Skye decided to go to his job and see if he was there or even worked the night before. She glanced over at Payton who'd fallen back asleep. She then walked back into the livingroom and woke Kareem up once again.

"I need you to listen out for Payton. Cruze didn't come home last night and I need to go look for him. I'm worried."

Kareem smirked, "There you go running behind another man. Where are you going to look for him at, the strip club? Tell Jordan to watch her, I told you I was tired," he said, with a smart tone. When he attempted to turn back over, she yanked his shoulder.

"Kareem, I'm tired of you disrespecting me. If you think you're gonna just come and go as you please and not do shit around here, you better think again! I'm sick of your self-ish, lazy ass!"

Skye knew Jordan had been going hard for the past few weeks in football practice and didn't want to wake him. But Kareem on the other hand never did anything to help her out and she was beyond sick of him not pulling his weight.

"Get the fuck off my couch! You bitched and com-plained about having your own room this time, so go get in your own bed!" Skye continued to roar.

Kareem sucked his teeth and jumped up snatching the covers. "You don't say shit when Cruze be sleeping on the couch," he replied, stomping toward his room and slamming the door.

Once again deciding to let Jordan rest, Skye chose to take Payton with her to Cruze's job. As her heart paced, she prayed he was there as she quickly got dressed and grabbed Payton out of the crib still in her pajamas and left the house.

Skye made the fifty-six minute drive to College Park in less than thirty. She was so anxious to get where she was going, the police pulling her over for speeding was the last thing on her mind. While driving, she glanced at all of the peo-ple out walking the streets and began to think about her prob-lems. She had so many thoughts in her head about whether she should go back to Miami. She also didn't like the strained rela-tionship between her and Kareem. Skye had let him get away with so much because of what he'd experienced the night Sandino was shot, but she was beginning to think he was using it as an excuse to be a loser and not do anything with his life. And that wasn't going down. All her kids were going to be successful if she had something to do with it. She also didn't know what was up with Cruze lately. All Skye knew was that she wasn't about to put up with any more bullshit from another man. Years of putting up with Sandino's lies and abuse were never going to be repeated.

When Skye finally saw the sign that said, Sal's Used

Cars she quickly turned into the parking lot and immediately noticed that Cruze's car wasn't there. She parked and grabbed Payton out the back of her black 2003 Nissan Maxima that Cruze bought when her Honda finally broke down. She remembered how proud Cruze was when he gave her the keys. She didn't want to hurt his feelings so Skye acted as if she liked it.

I should've been more appreciative because without him I wouldn't be driving shit right now, she thought.

Skye looked around and wanted to laugh at some of the old cars the dealership was attempting to sale. A gold 2007 Infiniti G35 was the nicest thing on the lot. She wondered if the cars were the new inventory Cruze had mentioned the day before. Skye couldn't even picture Cruze working there, but he constantly told her how cool the owners of the mom and pop dealership were and how they didn't judge him or the fact that he had a felony.

Skye walked towards the sign on a raggedy trailer that said office and went inside. The office was shabby, junky and smelled like moth balls. After seeing her reflection in a dusty mirror, she tried to finger comb her hair that was all over the place as an older man drinking a cup of coffee immediately walked over with a huge smile.

"I got the perfect car for you out back. It just came in yesterday and has your name written all over it. It's a 2006 Honda Odyssey," he said

"I'm not here to buy a car even though my boyfriend who works here told me about the new shipment of cars coming in. Is he here?" Skye asked.

"Who is your boyfriend? I know you're not talking about my crazy ass nephew. You're too pretty for Lamont."

Skye shook her head. "No, I'm talking about Dezmond. Dezmond Cruze."

The salesman looked at her crazy. "Who? Nobody by that name works here," he informed, taking another sip of coffee.

Skye stood there for a minute. "Are you sure Dezmond Cruze doesn't work here?" Skye looked around as if she expected Cruze to walk out of one of the offices in the back.

"Miss, I own this place, and I've been here every day for the past twenty years. I would know if somebody by that name ever worked here. I've had a lot of guys run through here, but ain't nobody ever worked here by that name." He took another sip of coffee. "Now, do you wanna take a look at that Honda? It's a beauty. Only got 78,000 miles on it."

"No, thanks," Skye said, walking out.

Skye left puzzled. Cruze had been claiming to go to this job every day for the past seven months and it was obviously all a lie. She could feel her temperature rising as she thought, *not again, I trusted this muthafucka!*

After opening the back door and putting Payton in her car seat, Skye hopped in the driver's side. She banged her fist on the sterling wheel with all types of thoughts going through her mind.

"My gut feeling told me something wasn't right. I bet that muthafucka is cheating on me!" she yelled. Skye started the car and pulled out the parking lot like it was NASCAR Season at the Daytona 500.

While driving, Skye started hyperventilating and having a panic attack. She reached over in her purse in the passenger seat while trying to keep her eye on road and pulled out her pills. When she twisted the top off, the pill bottle fell on the floor.

"Shit!" Skye said, while trying to reach down and grab them.

It seemed as if she'd only taken her eyes off the road for a second. By the time Skye looked back up, she could see two rear lights only inches away from her car. Going way too fast to stop, Skye let out a piercing scream as she hit the breaks but still managed to collide into the back of another car.

Chapter Eight

Skye was completely delusional as she laid in the emergency room badly bruised and cut. With everything a blur, she looked down at her clothing that was covered in blood and became hysterical.

"Where's my daughter?" Skye screamed.

When the petite Asian triage nurse working on her wounds grabbed on her arm, Skye started swinging back and forth.

"Ma'am, please calm down. I need to finish sterilizing the cut over your eye," the nurse stated. "Your daughter is with a doctor in another treatment area. From what the paramedics said you're both lucky to be alive. Your vehicle was completely destroyed."

Desperate to see her baby girl, Skye immediately jumped up off the hospital gurney and ran through the emergency room snatching each curtain back. She wiped the dripping blood from her forehead as she continued to look for Payton.

"I need to see my daughter!" she yelled.

"Miss, you can't disrupt the other patients like this. Come back and lay down, you need stitches. That cut is very deep and you're losing a lot of blood," the nurse said, running behind her.

Ignoring the Asian woman, Skye kept looking through various areas invading other patient's privacy in the ER until she finally found Payton. When she saw her precious baby laying on a gurney with her right leg wrapped in a splint and blood on her Dora the Explorer pajamas, she completely lost it. Skye ran to her bedside.

"Oh my God. Payton...Payton!" Skye belted. Flashbacks of the accident continued to flood her thoughts. "Is she okay?" Skye said, kissing her forehead.

When Payton started crying uncontrollably, Skye was even more devastated. Suddenly the doctor treating Payton walked around the bed and introduced himself.

"Hello, my name is Dr. Matthews. I'm one of the pediatric orthopedic surgeons here at Southern Regional Medical Center," he said, extending his hand. "I'm sorry, I haven't gotten your name yet."

Skye did a quick handshake. "Skye Washington. Is my baby going to be okay?"

"Can I speak with you for a second Ms. Washington?"

"Why...what's wrong?" Skye questioned with a concerned expression.

"I just need to speak to you for a second. Don't worry," the doctor tried to convince.

"I'm not leaving my daughter. Can't you see how upset she is?" Skye said.

The doctor reached over and pressed the button for a nurse. When she walked in a few seconds later, the doctor told her to stay with Payton for a few minutes so he could speak with Skye. When the nurse was able to quiet Payton down, Skye agreed to go.

"Mommy will be right back, baby," Skye informed. She knew something was wrong with her daughter when she didn't throw a temper tantrum like she did most of the time whenever Skye left her.

Jackie D.

Skye followed the doctor into a private area not far from the emergency room and quickly took a seat, anxious to find out what was wrong.

"Ms. Washington, your daughter's right leg has what is called a Growth Plate Fracture," the doctor said, getting straight to the point.

Skye's eyes instantly welled up with tears. "A Growth Fracture? What's that?"

"The Growth Plate is the softer part of your daughter's bones where growth occurs, and it's generally the weakest part, which is why it's so easy to obtain a fracture. It's a very common injury for kids during a car collision. Most likely, your daughter's car seat wasn't properly secure and that caused her to be thrown around in the car, shattering her leg."

As the doctor continued to speak, tears continued to stream down Skye's face. She immediately felt guilty.

"We're waiting for the X-Rays to come back, but I've been doing this a long time and I've seen this type of injury many times before. Unfortunately, surgery has to be done to put the bone back into the correct position. If the surgery isn't done, the injured bone can possibly become deformed. That unfortunately can cause her leg to become shorter than the other."

At that moment, Skye became frantic. "Oh my God. I can't believe this is happening. My poor baby. A fracture basically means it's broken right?"

The doctor patted her on the shoulder. "Yes, that's correct, but don't worry Ms. Washington, everything will be fine. This type of fracture can be corrected. Plus, things could've been a lot worse."

"Is it painful?" Skye questioned.

"Yes, I'm sure there's pain involved which is to be expected. But I've already given her something to try and keep her calm. Once we're able to sedate her, that'll help even more."

Jackie D.

"Where did all the blood come from on her pajamas?"

"She has a few minor cuts on her neck and collar bone which the paramedics said came from the shattered glass, but that's also nothing to be concerned about. Your wound, however, needs to be looked at."

"I'm fine," Skye tried to assure.

"No, I need you to go back and let one of the other physicians stitch up that cut. I'll come over and get you once we get Payton's X-Rays back. I'll need you to fill out some paperwork in order to proceed with the surgery."

"Yes, of course. Thanks, Dr. Matthews."

When the doctor left, Skye sat gathering her thoughts. Completely upset, it wasn't long before she broke down crying once again. The fact that she'd come out of the accident with only minor injuries, but her baby needed surgery weighed heavy on her heart. Skye couldn't believe that she'd let herself get so upset over a man that it had almost cost them their lives.

I don't know what the fuck is going on with Cruze, but he might as well consider this relationship over, she thought.

An hour later, Skye sat biting her nails with a huge bandage on her head while waiting for Payton to come out of surgery. After briefly talking to the doctor and confirming that his diagnosis was correct, they didn't waste anytime getting Payton into the operating room. Ever since Skye walked along side her daughter's gurney and watched as they wheeled her into the restricted area, she'd been on pins and needles.

Getting impatient, Skye walked to the back of the waiting room area to use one of the complementary phones. When one of the paramedics retrieved her purse from her wrecked vehicle, her cell phone wasn't in it, and neither were her pills. At a time like this, she really needed one to calm her nerves.

Jackie D.

Her heart was beating so fast it felt like it was going to pop out of her chest.

She looked around at one of the families in the waiting area. Seeing some of them laid out in the chairs made her wonder how long they'd been waiting for their loved one to come out. It was such a nerve wrecking process.

Skye decided to try calling Cruze once again. However, just like it had done all morning, the call went straight to voicemail, which had Skye seeing red.

"Cruze where the fuck are you? Payton and I were in an accident, and she had to undergo emergency surgery. Come to Southern Regional Medical Center in Riverdale A.S.A.P!" she said, slamming the phone down. She stood for a few seconds thinking, before dialing Kareem's number.

Maybe Cruze went home and fell asleep, Skye thought, as she waited for Kareem to pick up his phone. She tried her best to give him benefit of the doubt.

"Hello," Kareem answered in a groggy voice obviously still asleep.

"Is Cruze there?" she immediately asked him.

Kareem breathed in the phone as if he was irritated. "No. He's not here."

"Well, wake up, I need you to call him for me. His phone keeps going straight to voicemail."

Kareem immediately became irritated. "No, I'm not calling him. You need to stop sweating that nigga so hard. If it's going straight to voicemail that means he turned it off."

Her blood pressure went sky high as soon as she started yelling. "Look, I'm not in the mood to deal with your bullshit right now, Kareem. Payton and I were in a car accident. I'm in the emergency room. Now, do what I told you!"

Kareem's tone instantly changed. "In the emergency room? Are you guys alright? What happened?"

"I totaled the car. I'm bruised and banged up, but Payton is the one who really got hurt. She's in surgery."

73

Jackie D.

"Oh my God. What happened to her?"

Skye could hear Jordan in the background upset, asking Kareem if he could speak to her.

"Her leg is broken, and that's all I wanna get into. Right now, I need you to keep calling Cruze for me so he can come up here. I lost my phone in the accident so I'll have to keep calling you back. I gotta go," Skye said, ending the call when she saw a tall woman holding a clip board walking toward her. Moments later, the Amazon woman stopped directly in front of her.

"Excuse me, are you Ms. Washington?" she asked.

"Yes, I'm Ms. Washington," Skye replied. She was so glad no one had said Mrs. since she'd been there.

"Sorry to interrupt you. Could you follow me to the registration area downstairs? I need you to fill out some paperwork for your daughter Payton. I promise the process doesn't take very long, so you'll be back in no time."

Skye cleared her throat, "Yes, sure."

When they reached the registration desk a few minutes later, the woman told Skye to have a seat. She then passed her a clipboard along with some several pieces of paper.

"I need you to fill these out and attach your insurance card along with your driver's license so I can make a copy."

Skye's eyes filled with tears once again as she lowered her head. "Umm...I don't have any insurance."

The woman looked at her and sat back in her chair.

"Could you just bill me?" Skye questioned.

The woman took a deep breath. "We could, but the hospital doesn't like to take that route. What about her father? Could we possibly bill his insurance company?"

"No," was all Skye could mutter.

Obviously feeling sorry for her, the woman tapped Skye on her hand. "I understand, I have a daughter, too."

Tears fell on the paperwork as Skye filled it out.

"Don't worry. Just make sure you provide us with a cur-

74

Jackie D.

rent address so the bill doesn't come back undeliverable," the woman said with a warm tone.

Skye was not only embarrassed, but it felt like she'd failed her kids.

I can deal with being broke, but when it comes to my children's health and well being it's a different story. I know what I have to do, my kids deserve better, she thought.

After sitting in the waiting room for what seemed like forever, Skye could feel her body temperature increase when she saw Cruze walking toward her direction. He'd obviously gotten her whereabouts in the hospital from the information desk downstairs. The closer he got, the more heated she became. Skye turned her head and rolled her eyes.

When Cruze rushed over and sat down beside her, he moved Skye's hair back and examined the bandages on her forehead like he was the doctor. He then put his hand on her leg. She instantly pushed him away.

"I rushed right over when I got your message. Are you okay? Is Payton still in surgery?" he inquired.

Skye gave him a crazy look, right before going off. "You rushed right over, huh? If you would've rushed your ass home last night none of this shit would be happening right now."

"Baby, I'm so sorry. I didn't realize how tired I was after unloading all those cars last night. The fact that we had just got back from the trip to Miami didn't help either. I sat down on the couch in the back room at work and ended up falling asleep. I didn't even realize the battery on my phone had died either. I would still be there if my boss hadn't come in and woke me up," Cruze said, yawning.

Skye's eyes widened. She couldn't believe he was lying

Jackie D.

right in front of her face. "You're such a damn liar!" she yelled. Everyone in the waiting area looked at her even though she could care less. "I went by your so-called job. You've never worked there!"

Cruze looked around to see who might've been enjoying the shouting match. "Can you please lower your voice?" he pleaded.

"Absolutely not! Are you cheating on me, Cruze?"

"No baby, I would never do that to you."

"Well, where the fuck were you?"

"Can we discuss this later? This isn't the place or the time," Cruze said. The truth was he'd definitely fallen asleep working, but it was in his car, not at a car lot. He knew, however, Skye couldn't handle the truth right now.

"You better tell me some..." Skye stopped talking when she saw Dr. Matthews approach them.

"Ms. Washington, Payton's surgery went well, but I still want to monitor her progress over the next day or so. She's in recovery right now. You should be able to see her in about forty minutes. You'll need to limit any activity that might put pressure on the injured area. Also, she's going to need long-term follow up care. This is necessary to observe her recuperation and growth."

Skye put her hands over her mouth. She was so grateful Payton was going to be okay. "Thank you so much, Dr. Mathews. You've displayed such a caring attitude. I apologize for being so disruptive earlier," Skye said, wiping a tear from her face.

"You're welcome, Ms. Washington, and I completely understand. I'll come check in on her again before I finish my shift."

When he walked off, Cruze grabbed Skye's hand.

"Baby, you can relax now, the doc said she's going to be fine."

Skye immediately pulled away and looked at him. "I'm

76

Jackie D.

still waiting for you to tell me what the fuck is going on."

Cruze lowered his head. He could see the disappointment in her eyes. He had to tell her something. "Look, I had to step up and make some decisions on my own that will help all of us in the long run. I lied about the job because I know that's the type of dude you want me to be, but I'm just not the 9 to 5 type."

"What type of decision are you talking about, Cruze?"

"I can't tell you that right now but just trust me," he replied.

Skye's eyes became two sizes bigger. She couldn't believe he lied to her the entire time and now he refused to tell her the truth. They both promised they would always be honest with one another and Cruze had betrayed that trust.

"Well, since you were out making decisions all fucking night without considering me, I'm making one without considering you!"

Cruze looked at her with a puzzled look on his face. "What do you mean by that?"

"I'm moving back to Miami to take care of my husband!"

Jackie D.

Chapter Nine

Cruze followed Skye as she stormed out of the hospital and into the parking lot.

"Leave me alone, Cruze! Go back to wherever the hell you were last night!" Skye blasted. She was irritated at the fact that he even bothered to show up.

He was in complete shock after hearing her remark about going back to Miami and wanted to discuss it further. Furious, he grabbed her by the arm and slung her around.

"I know I didn't just hear you say you were moving back to Miami to take care of Sandino."

Skye quickly snatched her arm away as flashbacks of Sandino's abuse flooded her mind. She went ballistic. "Don't you ever put your fucking hands on me again! Ever!"

"So, is that what the meeting in Miami was all about? Why would you even consider going back to a nigga who tried to fucking kill you? I can't believe you would do this shit to me," he yelled in her face.

Skye gave him an evil glare for a moment shaking her head. "You can't believe I would do this to you? What about me? I don't even know who the fuck you are right now or where you were last night. My daughter is laid up in the hospital and all you can do is think about yourself. I don't even have

LIFE *After* A BALLA

health insurance for my kids. Do you know how that shit feels?"

Skye stopped shouting when she noticed the blinking lights from a security guard's car coming towards them. It wasn't long before a broad-shouldered guy got out and made his way in their direction.

"This rent a cop muthafucka," Cruze said to himself.

"Hello folks. I've received a few complaints about a couple arguing in the parking lot. Is everything okay here?" the guard asked.

Skye looked in another direction without saying anything.

"We straight. We just had a little disagreement, that's all," Cruze told him.

The guard looked at Skye. "Is that true, ma'am?"

"Yes, everything is fine. I was just about to head back inside to check on my daughter," she assured him.

"Alright," the guard said, looking them both up and down before getting back into his car. When he pulled off, Cruze directed his attention back to Skye.

"So, are we gonna finish this conversation?"

"It's funny how you want me to be open when it comes to what I'm doing, but your ass didn't feel the need to talk to me about whatever the fuck you were doing last night. There's nothing else to talk about, Cruze. Bottom line is, you're not gonna be in my life playing games and I thought I made myself clear about that when we first got together. Besides, neither one of us has a damn job and I have to be able to provide for my kids. What other choice do I have?"

"So, I guess the money I've been giving your ass isn't good enough, huh?" It was clear from his facial expression that he was pissed.

Skye gave him another evil look. "I guess not," she said before turning around to go back inside.

80

Le Le pulled up at Kareem's apartment after receiving a call from him telling her his mother and sister had been in a car accident. After hearing how upset he was, she told him she would be right over. Grabbing her charcoal grey Birkin bag, she got out of the car, and walked towards the building hoping Payton was okay. She could care less about Skye. Even though they'd only met once, it only took a few seconds to get on her bad side and Skye was at the top of the shit list. Approaching the door, she knocked twice before Kareem yelled for her to come inside. As soon as she turned the tarnished brass knob and walked in, Kareem quickly came over and planted a big kiss on her lips.

"Hey baby, damn I've missed you," he said with a smile.

Le Le stood looking at Kareem's bare chest. His 6'2 muscular frame that exposed the recent Enzo abstract tattoo she paid for covered his entire arm. To be as young as he was, he definitely had the body of a full grown man.

"I've missed you too my young stallion. Is your sister okay?" she asked, rubbing her hands through his curly hair.

"Damn, did you forget about my mother?"

"Oh…yeah. I'm sorry. How's she's doing?" she asked with an unenthused appearance.

"Both of them are fine. My sister is out of surgery and everything went well, but she still has to stay for a day or two."

"Aww. Poor thing," Le Le responded. "Where's your brother and that guy Cruze?"

"My brother is over at a teammate's house and I don't know where the hell Cruze is and don't give a shit. In fact he's the damn reason my mother was in the fucking accident in the first place. She was out looking for his ass," Kareem said slightly pissed off.

"Well, go shower and get dressed. I want to take you out to eat to cheer you up," Le Le told him.

"Sounds good, I'm starving," Kareem said, jetting in the bathroom and closing the door.

At that moment Le Le immediately started snooping around the apartment. Known to be nosey, she was curious to find out anything she could about Sandino Washington's family. Le Le couldn't help but wonder why Skye lived in such an average apartment complex since they were an ex NFL family. She also wondered why Skye wasn't smart enough to stack some cash away for a rainy day. After fumbling through a stack of mail on the table, Le Le opened the coat closet in the foyer and jumped back when a bunch of football equipment fell out.

"Oh shit," she said, quickly picking up the smelly grass stained shoulder pads, cleats and a helmet. Not finding anything interesting, Le Le decided to go into Skye's room next.

"I know it's gotta be something in here worthwhile, I can feel it," Le Le said, looking under the mattress. When nothing came up, she looked on Skye's dresser and frowned at the bottle of Brittney Spears perfume.

"Cheap bitch," she said, opening her small jewelry box on top of the dresser.

Le Le turned her nose up at all the cheap looking costume jewelry until she came across a diamond heart pendant necklace. It was the only thing she admired since Le Le herself had owned a necklace just like it at one time. She'd misplaced the beautiful piece of jewelry about a year ago.

"I should take it since she talked so much shit the other day," Le Le said until a picture of Skye and a man suddenly grabbed her attention. She picked up the crystal glass frame off of the dresser. "This must be Mr. Cruze."

Le Le studied him long and hard before noticing the Tom Ford blazer he had on. "I have to give it to that bitch...she does have good taste in men."

Le Le sat the picture back down and opened one of the drawers. While tossing several socks and t-shirts to the side, it wasn't long before she suddenly came across a journal. She stared at it for a few seconds before opening it and reading the first page. Within seconds she slammed the book closed and began to rock from side to side. She then grabbed the bottle of perfume and threw it across the room like a professional baseball pitcher. The strong stench of the perfume immediately entered her nostrils.

Le Le was just about to throw something else when she heard the shower water shut off. Thinking that Kareem must've heard the bottle crash up against the wall, she quickly stuffed the journal in her bag and headed toward the door. As soon as she walked out of Skye's room, Le Le bumped into Jordan who had just come into the house.

"What were you doing in my mother's room?" he asked.

Thinking fast, Le Le looked at Jordan with a straight face. "I was looking for another bathroom."

Jordan studied her body language as he turned around to go into the kitchen. She watched him as well from the living room that overlooked the small kitchen as Jordan grabbed a bag of chips and an orange Gatorade out of the refrigerator. He then placed the items under his arm and walked toward Skye's room still eyeballing Le Le. He knew something wasn't right by the way she acted.

"Stay out of my mother's room. She doesn't like strange people in there." He made his way toward Skye's bedroom and closed the door before making his way back into the living room. He stood close to Le Le and stared. "I'm watching you. My mother said it's something about you that she doesn't like and she's right," Jordan continued.

"Look, I told you I was looking for the bathroom now get the fuck out my face," Le Le said, clenching her purse tight and walking out of the door.

"Tell Kareem I'll be in the car.

Two hours later Skye sat slouched down in a chair inside Payton's hospital room with bloodshot eyes from all the crying she'd done. She stared, unamused at the old, corny episode of *Raymond* playing on the T.V. As tired as Skye was, she couldn't sleep or eat.

Getting restless, she got up and stared out of the hospital window in a zombie-like state. She thought about a hundred things at once, not knowing what she would've done if she'd lost Payton in the accident. The thought made a single tear race down her face. Skye wiped it away thinking about how much she loved her kids, and would do anything to protect them.

The craziest thing is, I left Sandino to make sure my kids had a better life. But now I'm going back for the same reasons, she thought.

She then drifted to Asia's scandalous ass. Just the mention of her name irritated Skye. She knew Asia didn't like kids and the fact that she went through an entire pregnancy and gave birth was strictly to get Sandino's money. *That poor little boy doesn't stand a chance with that bitch as his mother.*

Her chain of thought was suddenly distracted when Cruze walked into the room. His clothes were all wrinkled and it looked like he'd been drinking.

"What the hell are you doing here?" she questioned with a disgusted look.

"Skye, I don't want you to go back. I know I've done some things to make you upset, and I apologize for that," he mentioned. "I'm also sorry that I betrayed your trust," he said getting louder.

"Sssh. Lower your voice before you wake up Payton. I told you it's nothing else to talk about. You need to leave."

"No, not until you hear me out," Cruze responded. "I want you to be with me. It's crazy how you're considering going back to Sandino."

"And it's crazy how you didn't come home last night. It's crazy how I trusted you and you're turning out to be a liar just like Sandino."

"Is it about the money? If that's the case, then here you go." Cruze walked over to Skye and placed a wad of money in her hand. "That's where I was all night. Out making that."

Skye looked at the money. "Where the hell did this come from?" she questioned. Little did Cruze know, he didn't even have to say anything. "So, you're back in the streets after promising me you wouldn't ever go back?"

"I know I promised, but we needed the money."

"Well, didn't you think the best thing to do was discuss it with me first instead of lying? We made a pact to always be honest, no matter what. Do you know I could've killed myself and my daughter? None of this would've happened if it wasn't for you. I want you to leave!" Skye yelled, throwing the money back at him.

"But baby…I did this for us," Cruze pleaded.

"Leave!"

Suddenly, the nurse came into the room and looked at both of them. "I'm gonna have to ask both of you to lower your voices or you're gonna have to leave," she demanded.

"He was just leaving," Skye responded.

As soon as the nurse left the room, Cruze tried to appeal to Skye one last time.

"Skye, I love you. I've always loved you. Trust me, I did this for you…for the kids. I wanted to give you all the things you deserved," he said, gazing in her beautiful green eyes.

Skye was livid. "You're a piece of work, you know that. I trusted you and you lied to me just like every other fucking man I've had in my life. All men are just alike. I want you out.

I don't ever want to see you again!"

Chapter Ten

Asia put the baby in his car seat and jumped in her Chevy Tahoe, which she was ready to get rid of and upgrade. She was so paranoid that Sandino might've put a tracking device on her Hummer when she first left Miami, Asia decided to trade it in as soon as she got to Chicago. After sitting in her hotel room going crazy looking at the four walls and listening to the baby cry, she decided to go ride by Sandino's house. Curiosity was killing her and she had to see what was going on with Skye.

By now everyone knew about the shooting incident, and everyone knew that Sandino had gotten shot in Skye's new home in Georgia. Even though every news report was different, it wasn't hard for Asia to put the pieces of the puzzle together. Obviously Skye had finally left Sandino, and he'd obviously tracked her down in another state. What exactly led up to the shooting, was the grey area, but Asia wasn't concerned about that anyway. She was more concerned with knowing why Skye was at Toni Vaughn's office that day and if she'd moved back to Florida.

"It just doesn't make sense. If she left, then why was she here meeting with his lawyer? Maybe she's divorcing him," Asia said out loud. When Asia smelled something sour,

Jackie D.

she looked down and saw that the baby had spit up on her shirt. She instantly became furious. "Shit…this is a $300.00 dollar shirt! Even though it's old, I still have to take care of the designer clothes I have left until I can go on another shopping spree," she said, grabbing a napkin trying to wipe it off. "I'm so tired of this baby, I need a break!"

Ten minutes later, she reached Sandino's block. After turning onto the street, Asia slowed down making sure she got a good look. Approaching the house, she was shocked to see that the house was completely deserted and the yard looked horrible. The once well manicured lawn was now replaced with dead yellow grass and a front yard filled with weeds. Even Sandino's Mercedes Benz that was backed up in the driveway looked like it hadn't been washed in years

"I've never seen their house look this bad. I don't see a for sale sign in the yard so I can only assume that Sandino still owns it, and Skye is certainly not living here," she mumbled.

Asia always admired Skye and Sandino's six bedroom Palm Island estate, and planned to get her and the baby one just like it. Between her child support and money from any other nigga who crossed her path, she definitely would be able to afford it. Asia reminisced about all the times her and Sandino fucked in their bedroom when Skye was out of town for one of Jordan's games. He would make Ms. Petra and the rest of family leave out as well so the two of them could have the house all to themselves. Asia really thought Sandino cared about her until one night she woke up at his house with one of his boys on top of her fucking her as Sandino stood by and did nothing. She was so drugged up she couldn't fight him off and she wasn't even sure who it was.

After doing a thorough surveillance of the house Asia once frequently visited, she realized nothing was going on over there so she turned around and headed back to her de-pressing hotel. While leaving the expensive neighborhood, she visualized herself purchasing one of the many beautiful homes.

Jackie D.

"Maybe if I do that we can be neighbors, like one big happy family," she joked.

When Asia pulled up at her hotel shortly after, she saw a cute guy getting out of a brand new Porsche Panamera truck with thirty day tags across the street.

She licked her lips and rubbed her hands together with excitement.

"Oohhh, I can smell new money a mile away," Asia said with a smirk. When the guy suddenly turned around, she became even more excited after recognizing who he was. "Oh my God, that's Divine."

Asia checked her appearance in the mirror and quickly fluffed her hair before jumping out and running across the street forgetting all about the baby. Divine was an aspiring rapper out of Miami that she once dated. After finding out he didn't have much money she dumped him. But now it looked like he'd experienced a major come up.

"Hey, Divine!" Asia called out.

He looked at her closely before finally recognizing who she was. "Oh shit, what up, Asia?" he asked, giving her a hug.

When Asia hugged him back she almost melted from his touch. She hadn't had any good dick in awhile.

"You still finer than a muthafucka. Where the hell you been at?"

Asia smiled trying to pull her stomach in to hide her baby pooch. "I've been in Chicago for minute, but I'm back now."

"Oh yeah, well, that's a good thing,"

"Why is that a good thing? You kicked me to the curb remember?" Asia said.

"There you go, ain't nobody kick you to the curb. Your ass kicked me to the curb. You just couldn't deal wit' me bein' in the studio all night. A nigga couldn't concentrate on his career with you always actin' crazy. I tried to tell you to be patient cuz it would all pay off, but you wouldn't listen. Now, I

Jackie D.

got a record comin' out wit' Def Jam."

"That's great, Divine. I know that's always been your dream." She looked him up and down. He was still fine and looking sexy as hell with a body that was cut to perfection. Standing at 6'4' he had a deep chocolate complexion, with light brown eyes and a nice grade of hair that he wore in a mohawk.

As they talked a little while longer, Asia continuously batted her eyes and licked her lips flirting with him. She could tell he was enjoying every minute of it.

"I'm havin' a party here tonight," Divine said, pointing to the fancy boutique styled hotel behind him. "You should come through. We have some catchin' up to do."

Asia's eyes lit up. It had been a while since she'd been out. "Sure, I'll come by. But I don't want any beef from any of your lil' girlfriends."

"What girlfriends? I'm still waitin' on you to act right," Divine joked.

Asia displayed a huge smile. "We will see about that."

"That's what up, I'll see you tonight then sexy," he said, hugging her once more before walking toward the hotel.

As Asia watched him walk off, she remembered Divine having a big dick that he really knew how to use well. And with him signing with a major record label, the chances of him getting some pussy was definitely a plus. Asia knew once she spent a little time with him, the money she needed to move out the hotel and into a temporary one bedroom apartment would soon come. She was just that good.

When Asia finally walked back across the street to her truck the baby was crying. She became irritated thinking about all the fun she was missing out on by having to take care of a child. If it wasn't for him being her meal ticket to a better life, Asia would've surely gotten an abortion. She reached in the back and grabbed him.

"I'll be glad when your lil' ass go to sleep. I got some

Jackie D.

shit to do tonight."

Several hours later, Asia was dressed and ready for the party. Her black strapless mini dress that was embellished with sequins was guaranteed to turn some heads. Not only did she have a goal of chasing after Divine's new cash flow, she was also taking bids from anybody else willing to contribute to her dry ass bank account.

Asia checked herself out in the mirror one last time. She was having a hard time breathing with her girdle on, but had to make sure the fat on her stomach was tightly tucked away.

All I need is some money for a tummy tuck and I'm back in business, she thought.

Since Asia didn't have anyone to watch her son, she'd already breastfed him, made sure he was dry, then put him on the bed in between some pillows as soon as he fell asleep. Her plan was to keep sneaking out the party and running back across the street to check on him throughout the night.

"What could go wrong?" she convinced herself.

After fussing with her hair one more time, Asia finally left her hotel room and headed across the street to the party. As she approached the exclusive hotel, Asia watched as several nice cars pulled up to the valet. When she saw a black Maybach Exelero with tinted windows pull up she was speechless. As she stood watching, a tall, brown skinned guy with pair of Gucci Avaitor sunglasses got out. Asia never understood why people wore sunglasses at night, but nevertheless, he was still stylish, and she could tell he was cute. A few seconds later, his entourage arrived in two freshly detailed Suburban's. The tall cutie and Asia gave each other eye contact. He definitely had money and Asia admired his style.

"Sandino is my Plan A, Divine is my Plan B and I think

Jackie D.

I see my Plan C. But then again he's driving a damn Maybach so he might be Plan A," she chuckled.

They both continued to stare at one another until he finally took his eyes off her to give valet his keys. When the passenger door opened a light skin woman popped out.

"Why the fuck do you keep eye balling my fucking husband, bitch?" the woman ranted.

Asia moved her head back and forth like she was looking for the person the woman could've been talking to.

"Yes, I'm talking to you!" she yelled as if she read Asia's mind.

However, before Asia could respond, the tall cutie walked over to the woman. "Baby, chill the fuck out. I told you if you started that shit tonight you were getting sent home."

Asia laughed before strutting inside the hotel. She didn't have time to get into a cat fight over some nigga, especially one she hadn't even fucked yet.

I wonder if they're going to Divine's party? I hope I don't have to hurt nobody. I'm on a mission to seek cash tonight so all that other shit is irrelevant.

When Asia entered the plush art deco lobby it was nice and elegant. A far cry from the dump she was staying in.

I miss luxury hotels, Asia thought as she followed a small group of people onto the elevator to the roof top party.

When she got off the elevator and stepped onto the roof, it was a luxurious oasis that had a birds-eye view over the glistening Atlantic beach. She seemed to catch every man's attention as she navigated her way through the thick crowd.

Moments later, Asia watched as the crowd went wild when the DJ started playing one of Divine's songs off his new album. It wasn't long before she found herself moving to the music. She had to admit, Divine had skills, and it was definitely a song that was radio ready.

She searched the roof for Divine and finally spotted him near the DJ booth talking to the same tall brown skin cutie from outside. As soon as she walked over, Divine greeted her with a big hug.

"Asia, I'm glad you came. We poppin' bottles all night," Divine said before looking at her attire. "You look sexy as shit in that dress," he whispered in her ear.

"Thanks," she responded with a slight grin.

The tall cutie couldn't stop staring at Asia and she knew he liked what he saw. However, his pit-bull wife who had just walked up stared Asia down the entire time and she returned the glare right back at her.

"Excuse me for a moment," Divine said to the guy and his wife before grabbing Asia by the hand and heading towards the bar. Grabbing a bottle of Moet, he poured both of them a glass.

I probably shouldn't be drinking since I'm still breast feeding, but a little bit won't hurt, she thought. Asia raised her glass for a toast. "Here's to your new record deal," she said, touching his glass with hers.

"To my record deal," Divine mimicked. "I'll definitely drink to that shit."

Over the next few minutes, Asia sipped on her champagne and enjoyed meeting all the different people Divine had introduced her to. Asia could see a lot of the women cutting their eyes at her as she clung to Divine, but she didn't care. She was the one going to be with him tonight, so they just had to get over it.

As soon as Divine excused himself to go handle something, Asia knew it was time to slip out and go check on the baby. She put her glass down on the table and walked to the elevator and out the door. After quickly running back across the street, Asia looked down at her watch when she reached her hotel door. She'd been gone exactly one hour. When she put her key card in the door, Asia quietly eased it open and tip toed inside. He was still sound asleep in the same spot.

"That's a good boy," she said after making her way

Jackie D.

back to the door and closing it.

As soon as she walked back onto the rooftop a few minutes later, Divine instantly came over and handed her another glass of champagne.

"Where you been? I thought I'd lost you." When the DJ played another one of Divine's songs, he started doing a little two step. "Come on, let's dance," he said, pulling her to the dance floor.

Asia was finally having some fun as she and Divine danced three songs in a row. It had been so long since she'd danced, every move felt good. She held her glass up as Divine poured her more champagne. While Divine sat in one of the plush chairs with Asia in his lap, two of Divine's friends came over and pulled him away from her. Immediately getting upset, Asia had no idea what was going on or what that was all about until she watched as several ugly strippers pranced into the party. From their cheap looking dresses, clear sky high heels and oiled bodies, it didn't take much to know that's exactly what the women did for a living. As soon as the DJ played one of Uncle Luke's fast paced songs, the women immediately started taking off their clothes, which sent the guys into an immediate uproar. They all began pulling out wads of money, and soon started making it rain with nothing lower than a twenty.

Throwing back two more glasses of champagne, Asia watched in amazement until she couldn't take anymore.

"Fuck this. I look ten times better than those hood rat bitches. I refuse to let them get all the money while I just sit around broke," she said, reaching inside her dress and popping the snaps on her girdle.

She then stepped out of her dress and exposed a sexy black bra and thong before starting to do a little sexy dance. By the time she moved her hips in a circular motion and removed her thong, all the men went crazy. The faster they threw her money, the faster she scooped it up. The ugly strippers were pissed that Asia was stealing the show, but they kept

94

dancing. Asia was so drunk and into her dance moves she didn't even care that her stomach was hanging out. She also didn't care that her breasts had started to leak. Realizing that her bra was soaking wet, Asia kept going. She dropped down to the floor and did a split and pulled her left leg behind her head like a true professional.

"Oh shit! Shake that ass, Asia baby!" Divine shouted.

Asia kept up her striptease act until the song was over. And even though every guy in the room kept chanting the word, more, she decided to call it a night. After grabbing all her money scattered on the floor, Asia quickly put her thongs and dress back on, then blew the men an air kiss goodbye. She could care less how many of them booed her, Asia knew she had to get back across the street to check on her son.

When she staggered towards the elevator Divine ran after her. He was so turned on by her performance, he immediately gave her a long passionate kiss filled with lots of tongue as soon as she turned around.

"Asia, please stay wit' me tonight. I want some of that good pussy," he whispered.

Asia wanted him bad, but knew she couldn't stay. She pulled back and declined his offer, then made up a lie about her having an early morning appointment.

I don't really need him right now anyway since I made enough money to hold me over for a few days, she thought.

"Can I have a rain check?" she asked.

"You gone leave a nigga wit' a hard dick after the way you was movin' dem hips? Don't do me like this."

"I'll make it up to you Divine, but I have to go baby."

After exchanging numbers, Asia gave him one last deep kiss before heading off the elevator and outside. Intoxicated from all the drinks, she stopped and pulled off her heels before continuing across the street. When she finally staggered off the elevator and onto the floor her room was on, Asia could hear the baby crying to the top of his lungs.

Jackie D.

"Alright...alright, I'm coming lil' boy," she said, searching her purse for the hotel key.

However, before she could open the door, an older lady from the room next door, poked her head out.

"Is everything alright, that baby has been screaming for the past twenty minutes."

Asia looked at her and said, "Mind your business, bitch!"

Chapter Eleven

Asia sat on the edge of the bed counting the money she'd made from stripping at Divine's party.

Damn, this is almost a thousand dollars. At least I got enough to pay for this room a little longer until I can get some real money. I wanted to ask Divine for some cash, but I didn't want him to think I was only after his money, which I am, she thought. *I need to play that situation smart.*

When she heard the baby make a noise Asia looked over at him praying he wouldn't wake up. She breathed a sigh of relief after realizing he was still asleep.

"Thank God he stopped all that screaming after I fed him," she said out loud. "His ass blew my damn buzz after hearing all that mess. I don't know how much longer I can do this shit without a nanny."

After taking off her dress, Asia slid the baby over a few inches and got into bed with just her underwear on. Looking for a pair of pajamas wasn't at the top of her to do list, but flicking through channels trying to find something good on T.V. was. When she turned to VH1 and saw a rerun of her favorite reality show *Basketball Wives L.A.*, Asia put the remote down. She loved to see what insane things Jackie Christie was gonna be involved in.

"That bitch is crazy. Somebody needs to beat her ass for starting all that shit between the girls," Asia said, shaking her head.

She was just about to make another comment, when suddenly a loud knock at the door startled her. Instantly, she jumped up and wondered who it could've been since no one knew where she was staying. After tiptoeing over to the door and looking out the peep hole, to her surprise, the tall brown skin cutie driving the Maybach was standing on the other side. Glasses and all.

How the hell did he know how to find me, she wondered.

He knocked once again.

"I just heard you talking, beautiful. I wanted to come meet you without all the interruptions. Are you gonna open the door or leave me standing out here all night?" he asked.

There was silence on both sides until Asia finally yelled out, "Hold on for a second, I need to get decent."

"Get decent? Girl, I just saw you shaking your ass for cash an hour ago," he joked.

Looking over at her son asleep on the bed, Asia had to think fast. She didn't want him to see the baby. She'd learned the hard way in Chicago that having extra baggage was a turn off for most men. Coming up with a quick plan, Asia decided to wrap him up in the dingy hotel blanket, then walked inside the bathroom, placed him in the bathtub and closed the door. She then grabbed her money that was spread out across the table and put it away before walking back over to the door.

I'll just make it quick, get his number and holla at him later after I find someone to watch SJ, she thought.

Asia grabbed her robe off the chair before messing up her hair to look like she'd been asleep. She then opened the door with half her body in the hallway and the other half still inside the room. She looked him up and down.

"So, are you gonna let me in, beautiful? I can only stay

for a minute. I got people waiting on me."

"Sure, come in," she said in a sexy voice.

Asia looked both ways down the corridor as he walked past her making sure his crazy wife wasn't lurking around before closing the door. He walked in taking inventory of the room, then shook his head at the cheap looking pullout couch and table.

"Why is a pretty lady like yourself staying in a dump like this," he asked, looking at all her clothes thrown around the room.

"It's just a temporary thing until my place comes available," she lied. Scared that the baby might wake up, Asia had to make this visit short and sweet. "I'm really glad you took the initiative to find me, but I'm afraid this isn't a good time. I'm exhausted and have to get up early for an appointment in the morning."

When she yawned, he smirked.

"You didn't act like you had somewhere to be earlier the way you were drinking and performing at Divine's party."

Asia covered her face trying to look bashful. "Yeah, I know. I had way too many drinks. It's been awhile since I've drank so I guess it brought out my alter ego, who happens to be a stripper," she said as they both laughed.

"Well, I like both of you, the good and the bad side," he replied with a sexy grin.

An instant smile appeared on her face as well. Asia was mesmerized by the strong, rich man standing in front of her with his sparkling, platinum jewelry.

"I know you're wondering how I found you?"

"Yes, actually I am. Were you stalking me?" Asia joked.

"You could say that. I had one of my boys follow you when you left the party. I just had to come over and meet you. Oh, and get your number. I'll be back in town the end of the month and I would love to take you out," he said, moving closer and tugging at her silk bath robe.

"But how did your boy find out my room number?" Asia couldn't wait to curse the crackhead-looking, white man out who normally worked third shift at the front desk.

"Let's just say I have connections," the guy responded. "I know how to make shit happen."

Asia liked the sound of that. There was nothing sexier than a man with power. At that moment, she grabbed his phone out of his hand, typed in her number, then passed it back to him trying to make the meeting quick and productive.

"Just make sure your crazy ass wife don't get a hold of my shit," Asia said.

"Oh, don't worry about that," he replied. So, what's your name?"

"Asia, what's yours?"

He stared at her for several seconds without saying a word then he rubbed his hands over his goatee.

"You don't remember me, do you?"

Asia looked at him strangely. "No…should I?"

His nose flared as he walked up so close she could smell the Ciroc on his breath.

"Let me refresh your memory." At that moment, he finally took off his glasses. "Eight years ago, the Ritz-Carlton Hotel in Houston. You stole a lot of money that didn't belong to you."

As Asia looked at him again, her heart rate quickly sped up and her eyes bulged. It was Zoe. A big time drug dealer she'd taken over ten gee's from and left town. She couldn't believe that she hadn't recognized him before. He was no longer the overweight man she once knew. He'd lost at least a hundred pounds and now rocked a bald head.

At that moment, Zoe walked over and grabbed Asia by the throat.

"I knew I would see your ass again one day. When I saw you outside the hotel I almost lost it. I still wasn't sure it was you. I see you had some plastic surgery. New breasts," he said, squeezing one of them. "But when you started stripping at the party and I saw the huge tiger tattoo on your thigh, I knew it was you, bitch."

Before Asia could say one word or make a move, Zoe took his fist and delivered a powerful blow to her face, instantly knocking her to the floor. The blow had such an effect that she could see all sorts of stars. She could also feel her face immediately start to swell.

Seconds later, Asia felt him grab her ankles then drag her towards the bed. After ripping off her robe, along with her underwear, he threw her onto the bed, then leaned over her naked body. She tried to struggle and break away, but to no avail as he positioned himself on top of her confining her to the bed.

At that moment, visions instantly flashed back into her memory of how abusive Zoe used to be. During the short time she was with him he constantly beat her and when she saw the opportunity to leave Asia took it, along with his money as a bonus for her pain and suffering.

She cried and begged for him to stop. "I'm sorry for what I did to you, Zoe. Please don't do this," she said, sobbing in a weak, straining voice.

"Shut the fuck up, you heartless bitch!" he yelled back.

Zoe pushed her legs open further before lowering his pants and ramming his long, skinny dick inside of her. Asia tried to scream, but he quickly placed his hand over her mouth. When she started to fight, he punched her in the face again.

"Didn't I tell you to shut up!" he belted, landing several quick jabs to her stomach.

Zoe acted like a mad man as he continuously pounded her pussy with aggressive force. If that wasn't enough, he continued to glare at her and say all types of obscenities as he banged her insides as hard as he could. Tears welled up in Asia's eyes at the thought that he might kill her. She prayed he would finish and leave.

Asia thought about telling him she had a baby and to please spare her life, but she knew he wouldn't care. She'd robbed him and for the first time her past had caught up with her.

A few seconds later, Zoe growled when he felt himself about to ejaculate. Suddenly, he pulled out, aimed his dick directly toward her face, then splattered cum all over her nose and mouth.

Thinking that the horrible incident was over, Asia was startled when she heard the deep voice of another man in the room.

"Hurry up Zoe, let me hit that," she heard him say.

When Asia opened her eyes to see a heavy set man stepping up for his turn, she couldn't help but wonder how he'd gotten in her room.

"No...please...don't," she cried.

"Damn, nigga, why you nut on that pretty face? I planned to bite it, you know I have a biting fetish," the heavy man said, ignoring her pleas.

The heavy man then lifted Asia's legs as far as he could and forcefully stuck his big, black dick inside her nest. She could feel his body heat as he thrust in and out with rapid strokes. Luckily for her he was a two minute brotha, because she soon felt him shaking and then release inside of her.

"Damn, you got some good pussy you nasty bitch," he whispered in her ear. He then started biting on her chest. Asia moaned in pain as he moved further down biting her on the stomach, then to her thighs.

She could hear Zoe laughing until suddenly he said, "That's enough, crazy muthafucka. Let's go. That bitch should know now that it was a mistake to fuck with my money."

Following directions, the heavy man immediately got up and pulled up his pants leaving bite marks all over her body. Asia was in complete disbelief.

As Zoe and the man turned to make their way toward

the door, Zoe turned and looked back at Asia. "If you call the police you're a dead woman," he warned before walking out and closing the door.

Asia knew he meant business. Like Zoe said, he had lot of connections. Feeling completely violated, she curled up in pain and started crying thinking, *karma really is a bitch.*

LIFE *After* A BALLA

Chapter Twelve

When Payton was finally released from the hospital two days later, Skye smiled, thanking all the nurses who'd taken such good care of her daughter as she wheeled Payton down the hall of the pediatric ward in one of the infant CuddleBug wheelchairs. In such a short time, all of the nurse's had fallen completely in love with Payton and ran over to her saying their goodbyes. It was overwhelming for Skye as they got on the elevator to leave. She fought back tears while looking down at her baby girl thinking how things could've really taken a turn for the worse. Payton looked up at her all smiles with a little cast on her leg and holding a sandy colored teddy bear. Her outcome since the surgery had been great, but the doctor informed Skye that Payton still had a long road ahead in regards to the physical therapy needed in order for her leg to fully recover.

"We're going home, baby girl," Skye said, returning the smile.

When the elevator door opened and they walked off, Kareem and Jordan were waiting in the lobby. Jordan hugged his mother tightly as Payton's eyes lit up when she saw her big brothers. She reached out for Jordan and he immediately picked her up.

Jackie D.

"Be careful, Jordan watch her leg, baby," Skye told him.

Kareem looked at Skye as they walked towards the front door. "It's gonna be alright Ma. You just need some time by yourself to focus on you," he told her. For once Skye agreed with his advice. "Oh by the way, I forgot to tell you that Le Le bought Payton a new car seat," he stated proudly.

Skye's mood instantly changed when she heard the name. As bad as she wanted to say something about not wanting Kareem's girlfriend buying Payton anything, she decided against it. Her family had gone through enough over the past few days, so she didn't need the drama.

When they walked outside to Le Le's car waiting in front of the building, Skye took a deep breath. Since she had refused to let Cruze come back to the hospital to visit and even told him not to come back to the house every time he called, Skye unfortunately had to catch a ride home with the woman she really didn't care for. Skye was actually pissed about it, but had to deal with it for now.

After securing Payton in her car seat, Skye climbed into the back without speaking to Le Le or even giving her any eye contact. Skye knew it was rude since Le Le was doing her a favor, but she just couldn't bring herself to do it. To make matters worse before pulling off Skye reached inside her purse, took out some money that Cruze had given her a few days ago, and handed it to Kareem. She'd been holding onto it for a rainy day, and to her this day was pouring down.

"That's for the new car seat," she said, sitting back.

Kareem looked at the money and shook his head. "Ma it was a gift from Le Le, please don't start."

"Well, I appreciate it but we aren't a charity case, so give her the money," Skye insisted.

"I'm right here. You don't have to talk like I'm invisible," Le Le finally butted in.

Skye huffed. "I was talking to my son and I can see

106

your old ass just fine."

"If you going to keep disrespecting me in my own car, you can get out," Le Le replied.

Skye grabbed her purse and put her hand on the door handle to get out, but Jordan stopped her. "Ma, stay in the car, we need to get Payton home."

Skye looked at Payton and kissed her on the cheek. Jordan was right, getting her baby home was more important than bickering about petty nonsense.

Kareem rubbed Le Le on the leg. "Come on, let's go, baby," he said trying to defuse the situation.

Biting her bottom lip, Le Le pulled off even though she was still aggravated and wound up. During the ride to the apartment, Skye and Le Le constantly gave each other the evil eye though the rear view mirror.

"Why the hell are we going the long way? We're gonna get caught in traffic," Skye complained.

"Maybe I should've let you drive then," Le Le shot back.

Skye was just about to go off again when Jordan patted her on the leg. "Ma, please stop, we're almost home," he pleaded.

When they finally arrived several minutes later, Skye quickly grabbed Payton who had fallen asleep and got out purposely leaving the car seat behind.

"Ma, you left the car seat!" Jordan yelled.

"I don't want it, so leave it in her car!" she shouted back.

While Jordan did as he was told and ran to catch up with his mother, Kareem and Le Le sat in the car for awhile.

"Kareem, I don't know how much more I can deal with from your mother. No matter how hard I try to be nice to her she just doesn't like me. I do understand that she was pissed about catching us in her room that day, but I tried to apologize. I'm a grown ass woman and I don't appreciate her talking to me like I'm a child or some bitch off the street."

"I know she can push your buttons sometimes, but try and give her a pass this time. She's been through a lot lately."

"I know she's been through a lot, but I didn't do shit to her," Le Le countered.

"Trust me, I understand. That's why I'm gonna talk to her...I promise."

"You better because I don't deserve this."

By the time Kareem and Le Le finished their conversation and finally walked inside, Skye was in the kitchen opening up some Moscato wine. Moments later, she came out with the bottle and a glass in hand.

"Can you all order a pizza or something? After we eat, I need for us to have a family meeting. I need to discuss something important and it's for familyyyy only," Skye said, giving Le Le a nasty look.

"Ma, can you please get off Le Le's back? The cheap shots aren't necessary," Kareem tried to defend.

"Kareem, you're in no position to tell me what's necessary right now. You don't know what the hell I'm going through. Besides, this is *my* house and if I don't want her here I have every right to say so," Skye responded. "Now, I'm going to take a shower and get myself together while Payton is sleeping," she said, heading to her room.

At that moment Le Le realized that in order for them to get along it was probably best if she tried a more sympathetic and understanding approach.

"I'm gonna go apologize to your mother and make peace with her," Le Le told Kareem.

Both he and Jordan looked at her like she was crazy.

"I don't think that's such a good idea. As much as I would love for you and her to get along, I just don't think it's gonna work. When she gets in her moods like this, its best to stay out of her way," Kareem advised.

"Maybe she just needs a woman to talk to," Le Le said,

Jackie D.

walking towards Skye's room and knocking on her door.
"I'm going to make some popcorn and wait for the show," Jordan joked.

When Skye said come in a few seconds later, Le Le walked inside.

"Skye, I just came to apologize. I know we got off on the wrong foot, but I really hope that one day we can be friends. I really love Kareem and hope you can accept me as part of the family,"

Skye who was sipping on her wine and packing up all of Cruze's clothes quickly shook her head. *I know this bitch didn't just come in my room. Who does she think she's fooling with this nice girl attitude? I don't have any more energy to deal with this bullshit.*

"If you ever need anybody to talk to, I'm here you know like a good friend. All women need someone to share things with."

When Le Le finished with her wack truce, Skye turned and looked at her.

"No, I don't accept your apology and you will never be apart of this family, Le Le. You're way too old to be dating my son, and I don't like you! Now, get out my room and leave me alone!"

Le Le walked out and slammed the door thinking, *fuck this!*

At the same time Jordan fell on the floor laughing while Kareem walked over and hugged her. "I'm sorry, baby, but I told you. Just give her some time. She'll come around."

While Le Le left the house more pissed off than when she first arrived, Skye finished off her third glass of wine as she packed up the last of Cruze's belongings. When she looked around her bedroom everything about it suddenly reminded her of him. Skye didn't think she could ever trust him again and she certainly didn't want to deal with him anymore. As far as she was concerned, their relationship was officially over.

Jackie D.

She sat on the bed and removed her clothes before heading into the bathroom, and jumping into the shower.

Skye frowned as the hot water hit her bruised and sore body. However, it felt good to be able to finally take a shower since she'd only been able to brush her teeth since being in the hospital. While standing under the water, her mind was all over the place. She wondered how her sons were going to react to the news of her wanting to move back to Miami. She didn't mind hearing their concerns, but wasn't necessarily in the mood for their criticism.

"I know I vowed to never go back, but things are a lot different now. Sandino can no longer hurt me and it's time for that muthafucka to see what it feels like to be in pain," she said to herself.

After hearing Jordan knock on her door telling her the pizza had arrived, Skye finally got out. She checked on Payton who was still sleeping peacefully in her crib and joined her sons in the kitchen once she slipped into some comfortable lounging pants and a t-shirt. Jordan had already set the table and had two slices of pizza on the plate waiting for her.

"Come on and sit down before your pizza gets cold," Jordan said.

He was always so thoughtful making sure everybody was taken care of. Skye didn't know what she would do without him.

"Thanks baby," she said, kissing him on the cheek and sitting down.

Kareem looked at his mom like a jealous little boy. "How come you never treat me like that? When is the last time you kissed me on the cheek?" he questioned.

"Because you aren't as sweet and thoughtful as Jordan. You're too damn selfish and never do anything to help me out. Besides, you have Le Le to kiss you now," Skye responded with a light chuckle.

"Very funny," Kareem replied.

Jackie D.

As they all began eating, Skye told them a little bit about Payton's injury and how they had to be careful that she didn't start trying to run around like The Tasmanian devil again and re-injure herself. Once that briefing was over, Skye decided it was time to tell them the news.

"I have something else really important to talk to you guys about concerning our family."

They both looked up from their food with curious stares.

"Where's Cruze? If we're having a family meeting shouldn't he be involved?" Jordan asked.

"He's not our father so who cares if he is here or not," Kareem shot back.

As soon as the two of them started arguing, Kareem got up in Jordan's face.

Skye instantly became agitated. "Kareem, how many times do I have to tell you about your temper? Sit down and shut up before y'all wake up your sister. I'm so sick of you two always bickering like little girls. I can't deal with this shit right now!" she yelled, slamming her fist down on the table.

When her behavior startled both of them at the same time, Jordan quickly ran over and rubbed his mother's shoulder.

"Sorry Ma, we didn't mean to upset you."

A few minutes after things calmed down, Skye told them about the meeting with Sandino's lawyer. She also told them about Sandino having severe brain damage and not being able to handle his finances, so she'd been appointed to take care of everything. She went on to explain that in order for her to be able to provide for them they had to move back to Miami.

"I'll go wherever you and Payton are going, Ma. Are we moving back into our old house?" Jordan questioned in his normal calm demeanor.

"Yes, its part of the agreement. I have to stay married to

Jackie D.

him and provide care for him at the old house."

Kareem was quiet. Although he wanted to go back to his old lifestyle he didn't like the part about living with his father. He hated him and couldn't bear to be in the same house again.

"Count me out, I'm not going back. I don't want to see that dude. Just send me some money. I'll stay here with Le Le," Kareem said.

"Hell no, you're coming with us, Kareem," Skye protested.

Kareem didn't want to start another argument. He knew she didn't have her pills and he didn't want to send her over the edge so he just kept quiet thinking, *fuck that, I'm not going back to Miami.*

"Is Cruze coming, too?" Jordan asked. It was obvious that he really liked him.

"No, Cruze isn't coming. Actually he's not gonna be coming around anymore, and I'm not worrying about anybody but the four of us moving forward," Skye answered.

"Why?" Jordan questioned.

Skye sighed. "I really don't wanna get into that right now."

During Kareem and Jordan's argument, Cruze had knocked on the door. When no one answered, he used his key and quietly came into the apartment. He stood in the small foyer eavesdropping as Skye told the boys about her plans. Finally deciding to join in on the conversation he rushed into the dining room scaring them half to death. He then directed his attention to Kareem and Jordan.

"Listen guys, I know I haven't been around a lot lately and I apologize for that. I was out in the streets trying to make some money to take care of this family and give your mother the world. But I broke a promise to her. I was wrong for that, and I hope she will one day forgive me. I also hope that she'll marry me," he said, getting down on one knee and pulling out

112

Jackie D.

a two-carat brilliant cut diamond ring. He looked up at Skye with tears in his eyes.

"Skye, I love you and I'm so sorry for hurting you. Please…I want you to be my wife."

Jordan immediately stood up and cheered while Kareem frowned, stood up and walked out of the room. Meanwhile, Skye stood speechless for a few seconds. Her emotions were all over the place. She wanted to accept his apology and his proposal, but at the same time she was scared and hurt. She just couldn't trust him and wondered what other secrets he might be hiding from her. Skye had also made herself a promise after Justice betrayed her that if she ever gave her heart to another man and he deceived her, she wouldn't waste years trying to make that relationship work. She needed time to take care of herself for a change. If Cruze really loved her like he claimed, he would understand and wait. If not, it wasn't meant to be.

"I'm sorry, I can't take this ring. Your things are packed I need you to leave me and my family alone!

Jackie D.

Chapter Thirteen

FOUR WEEKS LATER

Skye stood at the top of the stairs gazing over the balcony, admiring the extensive changes she'd made to her old home. She especially admired the boldness of the now red and white living room. The red accent wall along the hallway was downright orgasmic. She sipped her wine and thought about why she'd chosen the daring color. It wasn't necessarily her favorite, but what made it sweet was the fact Sandino loathed red. In the past, he'd never let her wear it and he detested red lipstick. He would always say red was only for bitches and hoes, and then he would ask Skye which one she represented. She frowned at the memory. In her opinion, red represented power and strength, both of which she now possessed. And with her new found strength, it was time to show Sandino Washington who is in charge.

"He'll be pissed off, but what is he gonna do, run after me?" Skye said, with a smirk.

She was finally starting to feel at home after the transition back to Miami. With so many mixed emotions, bad memories, and negative energy the first night proved to be very difficult for her. After waking up in a cold sweat from constant nightmares about Sandino trying to kill her, Skye sat up for hours thinking that she had to make some changes to the house in order for her to move forward.

The next day she had a huge garage sale, getting rid of every piece of furniture including some of Sandino's prized possessions. From the garage sale money and the money she took out of Sandino's account, Skye went to work by hiring a professional decorator to come in and redo everything. Now, it looked and felt like she had a voice, which was something she'd never experienced.

Once Skye decided to move back to Miami, she called Sandino's lawyer and told her she'd decided to be his Power of Attorney. Within twenty-four hours, the lawyer had sent all the necessary paperwork via Fedex, and before Skye knew it, she was officially in charge of all his money. Skye smiled every time she thought about how good it felt to not have any more allowances...not to have anyone tell her what to spend and how much. It was the happiest she'd been in a while.

Spending money and buying things to transform the house gave her a rush, so since she couldn't fit any of the expensive clothes that were still hanging up in her huge walk in closet, Skye and the kids went on a much needed shopping spree. Besides, all the cheap clothes she'd brought from Georgia just didn't seem to go along with the lifestyle she was now reclaiming.

Her mind suddenly drifted to her kids. Jordan who was at school, enjoyed being back and had already talked to his former coach about getting back on his old football team again since the season had just started. Payton's injury seemed to be healing without any complications and she was scheduled to go see her new orthopedic physician the following week. She was even back to her old self again, smiling and trying to walk so she could get into everything.

Kareem on the other hand had stuck to his word and

stayed in Georgia. When Skye and Kareem had a long overdue conversation before she left, he finally broke down crying letting out all the pain he had bottled up inside from what he'd experienced over the years from all Sandino's abuse. After she continuously tried to get him to come with them and he wouldn't budge, Skye finally decided to respect his wishes. However, that still didn't hide the fact that it was hard to leave her son.

The whole Kareem and Le Le situation still bothers me, but the more I complain about it I'm probably pushing him closer to that bitch, she thought. *But I'm not giving up. I'll wait for a week or two and try to convince him again.*

Hearing the door bell ringing suddenly broke her daze. Skye looked at her watch and realized it was already 11:00 a.m. and time for Sandino's live in nurse to come and get things ready for his arrival later that day.

After being sleep deprived and walking around like a zombie all morning, she wasn't at all ready to meet Sandino's nurse. She sighed and put down her glass of wine and headed toward the foyer. When Skye looked out of the huge glass door, she was surprised to see a nice looking man standing outside with a suitcase. She cracked the door looking out.

"May I help you?" she asked, though the door.

"Hello ma'am, my name is Quinn Jacobs. I'm from HealthSouth Rehabilitation. I'll be Mr. Washington's nurse," he replied showing a small gap between his two front teeth.

She stepped back and opened the door. "Oh, yes I was expecting you. Please come in, I'm Skye," she said, introducing herself.

Quinn walked inside wearing a pair of navy scrubs with a body of steel. "Nice to meet you," he replied, rolling the black luggage behind him.

Damn, he's fine. He looks just like just Michael Jai White from the movie 'Why Did I Get Married' and he's built like him, too. This is a plus, especially since I cut Cruze off

*and haven't had sex in a while. It's going to be real good hav-
ing this eye candy around. I can see his big muscular arms
picking Sandino up out that wheelchair now,* she thought.

"Let me show you around, then I'll show you which
room you'll be staying in," Skye said, walking in front of him.

"You have a really nice home, Mrs. Washington," he
said, following her.

Skye could feel him staring at her ass as she walked
down the hall.

"Thanks, but please…call me Skye. I no longer go by
Mrs. Washington."

"Oh, I didn't know. I'm sorry about that."

"It's not a problem. I'm happy to correct people actually."

Skye showed him all of the work that the contractors
had done to make the house handicap accessible for Sandino.
This included building a wheelchair ramp outside, widening all
the doorways and transforming the downstairs bathroom into a
roll-in shower.

"Now, here's your room right here," Skye said, pushing
the door open. "Everything in here is new. New bed, new
linen, and a new fifty-inch LED T.V. I tried to make it as comfortable for you as possible, so let me know if you need anything."

Quinn smiled. "Thanks. Once I get unpacked I need to
check out you and Mr. Washington's bedroom to make sure
everything is up to code."

"Well, his room is right across the hall so you don't
have to go far." Skye pointed. "My room is upstairs."

Quinn looked somewhat confused. "Oh…okay well
that's cool. After I check on that, I'll come and talk to you
about my schedule and days off. We also need to discuss our
rotation in regards to taking Mr. Washington to physical therapy."

"Your days off? And who's taking that man to physical

118

therapy? I'm not doing that," Skye said, walking out of the room to go pour herself another glass of wine.

Again Quinn looked at her strange wondering why Skye stayed in another room and why she didn't want to take care of her own husband. *Let me mind my own business,* he thought. *My job is not to pry.*

Not long after, Quinn joined Skye outside on the patio and began to discuss Sandino's care. It was so many different things that came along with Sandino's rehabilitation, Skye was glad Quinn was well trained and handled all of it because she hadn't planned on lifting one finger. She was living up to her part of the agreement by being in the same house with him and making sure he was cared for. But that was as far as she'd planned to go. Skye even wished she could block off part of the house so she didn't have to see him.

Later that afternoon, Skye tried to lay down and take a nap, but still couldn't sleep. The nervousness of Sandino coming had her on the edge. So, instead of resting she opened another bottle of wine and continued to sip.

Suddenly chill bumps ran up and down her arm as Skye heard the beeping noise of a truck backing up. She looked out the upstairs window and saw a white van backing into the driveway that read, HealthSouth Rehabilitation. When her leg started shaking Skye wondered if she was going to be able to hold her composure when she saw Sandino for the first time in months.

"I hate that demon. He destroyed my life and I plan to return the favor," she said to herself, then looked in the mirror.

The nude colored Herve Leger dress she wore fit her now curvy size eight body like a glove. She'd been working out every day in the gym downstairs trying to relieve her stress and drop some pounds all at the same time. And it was working because she'd managed to drop most of the weight she'd gained while living in Georgia. Plus, she didn't have much of an appetite now since she'd moved back to Miami. Skye knew she was way over dressed, but she wanted Sandino to see what he was missing out on and how much he'd fucked up a good thing.

Skye watched as Quinn went out and greeted the other nurses transporting Sandino. A huge ramp on the side of the van was lowered down and a few minutes later, she saw Sandino's wheelchair being pushed off. Skye was shocked when she finally saw his thin frame and thick, full beard. He looked more like Teddy Pendergrass after his accident then Sandino Washington. It was actually scary.

As Quinn pushed the wheelchair off of the ramp and started wheeling him towards the house, Sandino looked up and noticed Skye standing in the window. While his eyes lit up like an excited child, hers were cold as ice. Sandino stared at her like he was hypnotized.

"When I get through with that muthafucka, his ass is gonna wish he really was dead," Skye said.

Once Quinn pushed Sandino's wheelchair into the foyer of the house, Skye stood at the top of the spiral staircase looking down with Payton in her arms. Her eyes widened a bit as she got a closer look at the frail man who no longer looked like the muscular Sandino Washington that she'd married years ago. To say he looked awful was an understatement when describing his appearance. In all her years married to Sandino she'd never seen him with any facial hair so the beard was beyond creepy.

After a closer view, he looked less like Teddy Pendergrass and more like a scrawny injured veteran returning home from the war. Or like a homeless man you see on the street. Watching him slouched over in the wheelchair dressed in an oversized army green sweat suit made her feel like she was looking at a complete stranger. Over the years of their marriage even during his abuse and drug use, one thing never changed. Skye could never deny the fact that she always found Sandino to be irresistible and sexy. But for the first time ever, that had definitely changed.

When she walked down the stairs, Sandino studied her up and down with his piercing eyes. She immediately began to think about all the promises he'd made to her that the abuse and cheating would stop, but each time it only got worse. Thinking about her constant pain, Skye actually hated Sandino for everything he'd done, and planned to show him just how much.

This shit is going to be harder to deal with than I thought. I wanna run over and kick his ass so bad just so he can see how it feels to be abused and belittled in front of someone. But now that the tables are turned, he will endure some of the pain I experienced. Payback is a bitch, she thought to herself.

As Skye walked down the stairs, a smile instantly formed on Sandino's face and his eyes lit up like a bright sun. He seemed especially excited to see Payton. She'd always been daddy's little girl and he was surprised at how big she'd gotten. Payton studied Sandino strangely with the beautiful green eyes she inherited from her mother. But then suddenly started crying as Sandino sat in his wheel chair staring at them like a mad man.

Skye purposely turned her back so he could no longer see his daughter. "Your scary looking ass hasn't been in here five minutes and you're already making us upset."

Embarrassed, Sandino turned his head and looked in the direction of the boys' rooms expecting to see his son's next.

Once again Quinn felt awkward as he cleared his throat. "Are you ready to assist me with helping Sandino get settled into his room?"

Skye sucked her teeth. "No, I'm not! I thought that's what you were here for. I mean… I made sure he had clean linen on the bed, what more to you want me to do? I'm telling you right out the gate, don't be expecting me to spend a lot of time in that room," she responded.

LIFE *After* A BALLA

Quinn looked at her funny. "Yes ma'am. Thanks for the heads up. Well, I'll be right back. I have to go help the medical supply company bring in some of the equipment needed in Mr. Washington's room. He's going to need a holster to help him in and out of the wheelchair along with a few other things," he said before walking toward the front door.

Payton was still whining so Skye took her upstairs to lay down for a nap. Seconds later, she returned and walked towards Sandino in an intimidating manner and bent down towards his face.

"Just so you know, it's a new day muthafucka. The old Skye is gone! Your controlling ass set it up so that I didn't have any other choice but to come back here. But I just hope you're ready to deal with the consequences," she said, letting him know she meant business.

She then took her finger and plucked him several times on the forehead really hard in the same manner he did to her on several occasions in the past.

"Do you hear me talking to you, cripple boy?"

Sandino's eyes bulged and he moved his head trying to avoid her screams.

"Let me take you on a tour of the new house," Skye said, getting behind his chair and pushing him into the living room.

She cringed when she saw that the hideous cut literally from ear to ear across his shaved head.

"Do you like the new red color in here? You've always said red represented hoes. I wonder if Asia had on red the night you fucked her and got her pregnant."

A huge frown formed on Sandino's face.

"Well, since you fucked one of my old friends, I don't feel bad that I fucked one of yours."

Once again Sandino produced an evil scowl.

"On with the tour," Skye said, displaying a devilish grin while pushing him down the hall. The heels of her new Gucci

122

sandals echoed loudly on the expensive marble floors as she made her way to the family room; a place that was formally Sandino's shrine. It used to contain all of his trophy cases and pro-football memorabilia, but not anymore.

"As you can see, I got rid of all that football shit. I sold it actually. And remember that nice ring you got from the 2008 Superbowl when you played with the Giants for that short time? Well, I sold that shit, too. That damn ring was worth a lot," she said with a chuckle.

As Sandino's eyes scanned the room, he started getting really agitated and making grunting sounds.

"I know you aren't about to cry, are you? I hope not because the Washington men are strong and not weak ass punks. Isn't that what you used to say to our sons almost every day?" Skye asked, taunting him with his own words. "What…are you pissed off because I destroyed a part of your life? Well, now you know how it feels."

Skye chuckled then slapped Sandino across his face twice.

"And shut up. That damn grunting noise is annoying!" she yelled in his face.

He stared at her. If looks could kill she would have been dead. Skye continued to push the wheelchair around the house showing him how she'd totally transformed every room.

When she approached Sandino's favorite area that he called his man cave, which Skye felt it should've been called his get high cave, she turned on the light.

"Remember what was in this room? Your expensive glass top Telovation pool table. Well, I sold it for little or noth-ing along with all the old furniture in the house. Too many bad memories were associated with all that shit," she told him.

At that moment, Sandino really started making all kinds of crazy grunting sounds. He was an excellent pool player and cherished the custom made $40,000 table. Sandino continued to look at her before closing his eyes as she continued pushing him down the hall.

"Now, this is my all time favorite room, it's called the all about Skye room."

She turned the knob and opened the door to what used to be Sandino's office and pushed him inside. It now had a custom designed mahogany desk with a top of the line Apple computer.

"This is now my office. I'm going back to school and finish getting my degree in Fashion Merchandising. I put my education and career on hold to be a supportive wife, but now I'm getting ready to do what I need to do for me." She got in his face again and tapped her chest. "For me! I'm fulfilling all my dreams that you felt weren't important, like my new shoe line that'll be launched at your expense of course."

Once Skye turned his chair around and turned off the light, Sandino didn't make any more sounds, he just looked straight ahead as if he was in a daze.

"Well, the tour is over. I hope you like all the modifications to the house. But then again I don't give a fuck whether you do or not. Oh yeah I almost forgot, since you can't drive anymore its no need for you to have five cars. I'm planning on selling all your cars. But then again, maybe I'll keep one of them and let your cute ass nurse use it to drive you back and forth to physical therapy," Skye said, pushing Sandino back into the foyer just as Quinn finished loading all the equipment inside his room. She reached over and whispered one last thing in Sandino's ear.

"Oh yeah, thanks for the brand new car. I have to go sign the paperwork and pick it up later," she informed him.

Quinn walked up and he wiped the sweat off his forehead. Skye admired his gorgeous body, but quickly brushed it off. She wasn't interesting in getting involved with another man right now, but she had to admit, there was nothing wrong with looking.

When Quinn noticed that Sandino's demeanor had completely changed he became concerned. Sandino's face was so tensed Quinn could see the veins protruding from his forehead.

"What's wrong with Mr. Washington?" he questioned.

There was a long period of silence between them. Skye sighed deeply.

"How the hell should I know? You've been the one been taking care of him, right? Maybe he's just glad to be home and overexerted himself," she finally responded.

"Yes, I've been working with him a few weeks before he was released. So maybe you're right. I guess being home after so long is a lot for him to deal with. And for you as well," Quinn said, grabbing the wheelchair and heading to Sandino's room.

Skye followed Quinn and stood in the doorway. She watched as he lifted Sandino out the chair and into the bed. She noticed his crisp white Calvin Klein tight fitting brief underwear when he bent over.

Damn, I would love to see what he's working with, she thought watching him closely as he performed his duties.

"You can come over and help if you like."

"No, I'm good over here. That's what you get paid for."

"Yes, but you really need to know how to do all this just in case I'm not here one day," Quinn advised.

"Well, if you're not here, I'm not pulling my back out trying to lift his ass. Matter of fact, I need to get a back up nurse just in case."

"Skye, can I tell you something?"

Skye shook her head. "Of course."

"I know its hard dealing with a love one injured to this degree. But part of Sandino's rehab and him getting on the road to recovery is to have positive people in his corner. I'm sure if the roles were reversed he wouldn't hesitate to help you."

Skye became pissed instantly.

"Quinn, I'm glad you think you know so much about

Sandino Washington. But let me tell you something. I have been a damn good wife and devoted my life to that man for almost eighteen years. I supported him and continued to stand by his side after every stupid stunt he pulled in our personal life as well as his career. Any other woman probably would've walked out on him a long time ago. He's always been the type of man who doesn't give a fuck about anybody but himself and if he wasn't paralyzed right now he would probably have his fist to my face. You have no idea what I've been through, so don't tell me what I need to do in regards to that muthafucka," she said, pointing at Sandino. "Next time, stay in your place, mind your business and remember who pays your salary. I'm the queen of this castle. All you need to be concerned with is making sure you keep him out of my fucking way," Skye said, walking out the room.

Chapter Fourteen

Several weeks had passed and life hadn't gotten any better for Asia as she sat on the balcony of her low budget hotel room. With visions of being raped still freshly etched in her mind, she poured herself some cheap Vodka inside an old McDonald's cup.

Not only did Zoe violate her in the worst way ever, she also realized he robbed her as well. To add insult to injury, he even took it a step further by continuously calling her cell phone and saying he was coming back for more. Terrified, and knowing that he wasn't joking, Asia quickly packed up and fled the hotel with her son in tow and rode around for hours bleeding, bruised and distraught.

Thinking back on the ordeal she poured herself another drink as a tear ran down her face. "How did my life get to this point?" she asked herself.

After deceiving so many people, Asia didn't have anybody to call in her time of need. The only person that she could think of was Divine, but after calling him several times hoping he could loan her some money, he never answered or returned her calls.

Desperate and broke she ended up at a pawn shop getting money for several pieces of her jewelry. She then had to budget the little bit of money they gave her on pampers, food and another hotel room. She'd called Sandino's lawyer at least five or six times to see if he'd taken the paternity test, but was forced to leave messages for the unavailable attorney each time. So far, no one had returned Asia's call and her money was running out.

Asia's mind suddenly drifted to her mother. She missed her so much, when she was murdered ten years ago, part of Asia died with her. After her father walked out on them when she was nine years old and they eventually lost their house and were living in the car, her mother vowed that once she got back on her feet she would never trust another man again. She said she would use any and every man that came in her path and she did just that.

Asia actually remembered the first time she saw her mother stealing money out of one of her boyfriend's pockets. She made Asia stand as look out while she took his money and bank card. Her mother had tons of different men going in and out of her life, and if he she met one who wasn't paid she wouldn't give them the time of day.

They finally hit the jackpot when Asia's mother met Rodney, one the biggest drug dealers in Texas. He fell madly in love with her and soon they were living in his 13,000 square foot home in the expensive River Oak subdivision. Life was good and Rodney spoiled them beyond anyone's wildest dreams. Asia thought her mother had finally softened up about her perception of men. That was until Rodney was busted by the Feds and got sentenced to twenty years. A week after his sentencing her mother moved on and started sleeping with his friend who had even more money. Her lack of commitment was beyond foul. She taught Asia everything she knew about manipulating men and Asia had been following in her mother's footsteps ever since. However, Asia felt like since she'd gotten pregnant and had the baby she wasn't on her game.

"I can turn this shit around if everybody would just stop

Jackie D.

plotting against me," she said to herself.

Asia had somehow convinced herself that she was entitled to the same thing Skye received and was determined that Sandino was going to pay her at least three or more thousand a month for child support.

She poured herself another cup of vodka and tossed it back. Since the rape, it felt like she was possibly becoming an alcoholic, but drinking kept her in a state of relaxation with all that she'd been though and with the baby constantly crying. At that moment Asia had to wonder if her son's cranky moods were caused as a result of her tainted breast milk.

Deciding to call Sandino's lawyer again, Asia grabbed her cell phone off the table and dialed the number. Prepared to leave another message, she was surprised when she finally heard a live person answer.

"Toni Vaughn's office, how may I assist you?" a new voice answered.

Asia put on her professional voice. "Yes, is Ms. Vaughn available?"

"May I ask who's calling?" the woman asked.

"This is Mrs…Washington. Mrs. Skye Washington," Asia lied.

"Oh hello, Mrs. Washington. I was just about to call you. We realized you accidently missed initialing one of the pages on your husband's paper work."

Asia paused realizing that this lady must've been new and really had her mixed up with Skye so she played along.

"What paperwork are you talking about?"

"The Power of Attorney paperwork, you know… making you in charge of your husband's money and estate. Ms Vaughn really needs you to come in A.S.A.P. Since you already have access to all his accounts, we just need you to initial that one final page so we can file the paperwork away correctly."

Asia's couldn't believe what she was hearing. Her temper boiled. Here she was struggling while Skye was getting the royal treatment.

"Okay," was all Asia could say.

"I know you're glad all the renovations to the house are finished," the woman continued.

"Yes, I am," Asia responded.

"I hope you and your family are finally getting settled back in Miami. That cute little girl of yours is so adorable. If you ever need a babysitter just let me know," the chatter box went on to say.

Asia couldn't believe how unprofessional the woman was, but was glad she provided her with that bit of information.

"I will defiantly keep that in mind. Is Ms. Vaughn in?" Asia asked.

"No, she's in court and won't be in until later."

"Okay, I'll stop by to see her tomorrow."

"Bring my baby with you," the woman responded.

Asia ended the call thinking, *I'll have a baby alright, but it won't be Payton.* She slammed her phone down on the table beside the lounge chair. After sitting there pissed for a few seconds, Asia started talking to herself.

"This is some bullshit. Here I am broke, eating fucking fast food everyday so Sandino's son can have pampers and Skye is obviously set for life! What the fuck is taking so long . with me getting my damn money?"

Furious, she started pacing the floor and mumbling under her breath. The revelation was a devastating blow as she punched the cheap mirror that was hanging on the wall in frustration. Blood splattered everywhere as several pieces of glass pierced her skin.

"Shiitttt!" she yelled out loud.

Disappointed and pissed, Asia looked at the reporter's card sitting on her nightstand as she turned around to make her way to the bathroom. She smiled as she grabbed a towel off the rack and wrapped her hand.

She walked out the bathroom, retrieved her phone off the table and picked up the reporter's card. After looking at it for a few seconds, Asia dialed the number on the card. When the call went to voicemail she left a message.

"Hello, my name is Asia Jones, and I think I have some photographs you might be interested in publishing. Please call me back when you get this," Asia said, providing her phone number and ending the call.

"It's time to turn this shit up another notch."

Kareem was slightly irritated as he rode in a cab listening to the African driver talk loudly on his cell phone in his foreign language. Trying to drown out the noise, he reached into his backpack, grabbed his OVO headphones and started listening to Drake's new album *Take Care*. He was headed back to Le Le's after storming out earlier that morning from another one of their huge arguments. Kareem just couldn't seem to do anything right lately and he was beginning to wonder if moving in with her was such a good idea. He felt bad about yelling at her, but Le Le was starting to get on his nerves by asking so many questions about why his mother left and where she'd gone. It was hard enough for him to deal with his family leaving yet alone getting the third degree about it. He was very close to his family and even though he and his mother didn't get along at times, she was his rock and truth be told he was lost without her.

They shared a very emotional conversation before she left about his feelings towards his father. She'd even held him tight as they both cried together. He felt a burden had been lifted and both of them telling each other their true feelings

Jackie D.

was the best therapy he could've ever had. It was a major breakthrough, and truth be told Kareem missed his family desperately. He couldn't wait to see them again. But until he could go to Miami and pay them a visit, Le Le was his family. Kareem knew he'd put up a shield and needed to open up more, so he was on his way to apologize for being so cold towards her.

When the cab pulled onto her street, Kareem noticed a car backing out of her drive way. Instead of stopping, he told the cabbie to keep driving past the house. When the car passed them, Kareem glanced over at the man who didn't see him. He looked familiar and so did the car. After instructing the driver to turn around and pull in her driveway, Kareem paid the fare, headed to the door, inserted the key, and walked inside.

When Kareem didn't see Le Le in the living room, he walked towards her bedroom, but stopped once he realized she was inside her closet talking. It was something he'd heard her do in the past, which had him wondering if that's where she liked to talk on the phone. As soon as he walked up behind her, she turned around completely startled.

"Who are you talking to?" Kareem asked, looking around like he expected to see someone. "And why are you always talking in the closet?"

"How did you get in the house?" Le Le asked ignoring his questions. "I didn't hear you ring the doorbell."

"I took your key, is that a problem?"

"Yes it is…a big problem. If I wanted you to have a key I would've given you one," she said. "Just like it's a problem with you being in my closet. You know this area is off limits." After Kareem made his way out, Le Le quickly turned the light off, and locked the door only wearing a thin, silk robe.

Kareem looked at her up and down furious, then wondered why she wasn't dressed.

"Who the fuck was that nigga I just saw leaving here? And why don't you have any clothes on?" he asked pissed off.

Jackie D.

Le Le immediately rolled her eyes. "I know you're not coming back in here asking me fifty thousand questions after the way you acted this morning. If you must know, that was my cousin. He's in town visiting and stopped by to see me. Why, what's the big deal?"

Kareem looked at her funny, squinting his eyes.

"Why you looking at me like that? You don't believe me? Do you want me to call him back and introduce him to you?" she questioned with an attitude.

"No, if you say it was your cousin then that's who it was," Kareem said, following her into the living room.

They both went over and sat on the couch.

"Look, I need to apologize to you about storming out earlier, but seeing that nigga pulling out your driveway got me all fired up again."

"Well, I'll accept your apology this time, but don't make that shit a habit. Just because your mother let's you talk to her any kind of way doesn't mean I'm going to." When Kareem shook his head, Le Le finally smiled. "Now, come here and give me a hug."

Being in Le Le's arms always seemed to make things right, Kareem thought as they embraced. He then planted a huge kiss on her lips.

"I love to make up," she continued. "It's the best part about fighting."

"Me too. You know my mother's ex-boyfriend used to have a car just like the one your cousin was driving," Kareem added.

"Oh really. So, who was your mom's ex boyfriend?"

"Nobody important. Just a low life muthafucka named Justice who double crossed us."

"Double crossed you? How?"

"He claimed to be so in love with my mom, but called my father and told him where to find us just to collect money because he was in debt."

Jackie D.

This information took Le Le by surprise. "Hold up, he called your father? What happened once he called him?" Le Le couldn't believe Kareem was finally being so open. The anticipation of him answering her questions was almost too much to handle.

"Look, I don't want to keep talking about that shit," Kareem said trying to change the subject.

Le Le stomped her foot in frustration. "Why do you get so damn defensive and shut me out when I ask you questions about your family?"

"I just don't like people asking me a lot of questions," Kareem responded.

Le Le took a deep breath. "So, I'm just *people* now? You know what, since you obviously don't think I'm trustworthy enough to learn a little about your precious family, but I trust you enough to stay in my fucking house, you should think about moving out," she said, walking off with an attitude.

Chapter Fifteen

Le Le circled the block several times looking for a parking space before she finally found one. After checking her cell phone and realizing there were ten missed calls from Kareem, she finally got out and walked toward the building. When she entered the coffee shop, the aroma of several different types of gourmet coffee lingered in the air.

"Welcome to The Singing Bean, can I interest you in one of our homemade deserts?" a lady behind the counter asked.

"No thanks, maybe later," Le Le said, looking around. The place wasn't very big, but the relaxed atmosphere was nice and cozy. She made her way past several people who all had their laptop computers out and walked toward the back.

"Why the hell did I have to call you so many times today before I finally got a call back?" she asked the person she was there to meet.

"Well hello to you, too, my wonderful sister-in-law," Dre said sarcastically. She hadn't even given herself time to sit down before going off.

After noticing that he'd already ordered her a cup of coffee, Le Le sat down, grabbed the cream and a spoon, then started stirring it into the cup. At that moment, she realized Dre was wearing one of her husband's Polo shirts, which instantly sent a cold chill over her body. Other then the fact that Dre was 6'4, two-hundred and eighty pounds with a tattooed body, compared to Justice who was 5'10 with a smaller build they looked so much alike.

"What's up Felicia?"

"It's so good to hear you call me Felicia. I'm so tired of going by that ghetto ass Le Le. This hood shit is definitely not for me," she stated, sipping her coffee.

"How could I forget, Ms. Bougie."

"I'm not bougie. I grew up in the projects like everybody else. I just don't go around acting like a damn fool. Besides, it's not my fault that I went to school instead of a strip club."

"Okay, Dr. Mitchell. Calm down," Dre said.

"Well, don't go there with me then. I'm proud to be a plastic surgeon. I worked hard to get where I am," Felicia boasted.

Dre quickly changed the subject so she wouldn't go on and on. "So, why did you want to meet me again after I just saw you?"

"Because I told you coming to my house was a bad idea, that's why. You almost fucked up everything. Kareem saw you leaving."

"So what. He doesn't know who I am. Besides, I already told you him livin' there was a bad idea anyway. I'm tired of stayin' at that fuckin' hotel," Dre responded with an attitude.

At that moment, Felicia reached inside her purse. "Well, how else would I have continued to get information if I'd let him move to Miami? Speaking of hotels here's some cash to hold you off for a couple more days. I forgot to give it to you earlier," she said, handing him some money.

Dre grabbed the four hundred dollar bills and looked at her long and hard, before throwing the money back across the table.

"That's the problem. It doesn't seem like you're gettin' any information. It seems like you're actually enjoyin' him bein' around. I hope you didn't forget that you got a fuckin' job to do. You better not be fallin' for that nigga. I went through too much trouble trackin' him down to have *you* fuck things up."

"Dre, please. I only love one man and it damn sure ain't Kareem. Don't try to play me. You did your part, now let me do mine," Felicia demanded.

"When I found his name on those papers Justice had at the shelter from the day he bailed him out of jail, I had to go to his court date, hide in the back of the court room and follow his ass to work. That's when I sent you after him. So, you better not fuck up this plan. My brother has been missin' for eight fuckin' months. I know he's dead and the police ain't doin' shit to help solve his case, so we have to find out if they had something to do wit' his disappearance," Dre protested.

"Don't you think I know all that? Do you know how hard it is to know that my husband is more than likely dead? I refuse to even have a memorial service until his body is found. Justice and I had plans on getting back together, and now that's never going to happen." Felicia could feel herself about to tear up. "Justice told me that he'd found a way to pay me back for all my money that he'd gambled away. He told me he'd changed, and I believed him."

Dre couldn't help but wonder if the money Justice was referring to had anything to do with Sandino.

"Do you know how hard it was for me to see that bitch Skye for the first time? I wanted to kill her with my bare hands, especially when I found that journal with her talking about how much she loved Justice. Since I'm convinced that she's responsible for Justice's disappearance seeing her makes my blood boil. I know what I'm doing, Dre. It's been a struggle, but Kareem is starting to open up. He even got so angry after an argument with his mother one day that he started mumbling something about a murder. I kept asking him what he was talking about, but he caught himself and tried to play it off. He's definitely hiding something, so it's only a matter of time before he tells me what happened," she informed.

"Alright, but just remember you're supposed to be gettin' information from him not fuckin' him," Dre responded.

Felicia caught a serious attitude. She didn't appreciate him trying to tell her how to handle her business. "I know what I'm supposed to be doing, and even if I am fucking him, it's none of your business."

"I'm just sayin', why you got the young nigga up in your crib now when you could be fuckin' me, a real man?"

Felicia sighed. "Listen Dre, what happened with us that one night was a mistake. I was just vulnerable. Shit, we were both vulnerable. Let's just forget it ever happened. I'll always love Justice and you're his brother, so it's wrong. Also, I gave you permission to drive his car, but I didn't give you permission to wear his clothes. That's very disrespectful by the way."

Felicia's mind suddenly drifted back to when the police found Justice's car outside of an abandoned warehouse in Alpharetta one month after they reported him missing. As hard as it was to come to terms with it, finding his car was confirmation that her husband was more than likely dead. He loved his BMW more than life itself and never liked anyone to drive it. Felicia also remembered when she went to Justice's apartment to gather all his belongings. She was devastated when she found a picture of Skye next to his computer, and fought back tears while packing up all of his clothes. Felicia took a deep breath before getting up to use the bathroom. As she walked away, Dre couldn't help but look at her plump ass when she stood up in her body hugging Miss Me jeans and embellished tunic. Felicia was a bad bitch and he never understood why his brother cheated on her.

Dre remembered the night Felicia came to bail him out of jail after he tried to reach Justice for over a week. She was

138

upset about not being able to find Justice and he was upset that Mercedes had gotten him locked up for raping Skye. The two of them rode around for hours trying to find Justice. After coming up empty handed, they ended up comforting one another followed by some drinks and eventually one thing lead to another. At first Dre felt bad about sleeping with his brother's wife, but he felt a sense of revenge at the same time for Justice sleeping with Mercedes.

I was so pissed with Mercedes for what she did to me. Shortly after my brother went missing, her body was found down in that embankment. I felt bad that she'd been murdered and left by the side of the road like that. I know she snuck and contacted Sandino behind my back to try and get money for telling him where Skye was, but I just hope that wasn't what cost Mercedes her life, he thought.

When Felicia walked back to the table a few minutes later and sat down, Dre started asking her questions about Skye.

"So, any up to date information about Skye?"

"No. All I know is that she moved from Lawrenceville back to their house in Miami. Kareem hasn't talked to her much since she moved, but I'm sure that'll change. I think he misses his family."

"So, where does he think you're going when you leave for work, Dr. Mitchell? I know you took a vacation when he first moved in, but what about now?" Dre questioned.

"Well, I told him I was a real estate agent, and luckily he hasn't asked me too many questions about it."

"Questions or not, you need to hurry up and rap this shit up before I have to get involved. This shit it takin' way too long."

"I told you don't rush me," Felicia countered.

Dre shook his head. "Don't forget I gotta go back to court in the mornin' for that bogus ass rape charge. My lawyer said it looks good for me and that the case will probably be thrown out for lack of evidence."

"Yeah, you have one of the best lawyers in Georgia," Felicia reminded him.

"By the way, I never thanked you for hookin' me up with this lawyer."

"You're welcome. But once this is all over I think we need to go our separate ways," Felicia said, getting up. She grabbed her Chanel messenger bag and placed it over her body. "Since we already crossed the line once it's only right. I'll let you keep your key until then."

"If that's what you want. In the meantime, just get movin' wit' Kareem's ass!"

When Felicia got outside, she headed towards the parking lot but stopped to glance at her husband's car. Happy memories of the day she purchased the BMW 760 LI for his birthday years ago instantly floated through her mind. Felicia began to tear up as she stood in a daze picturing them riding in his car while listening to his favorite Jay-Z CD. Justice was more than likely gone and she needed to try and move on with her life, but it was gonna be hard. The tears started flowing as she headed to her truck. Once inside Felicia completely lost it. She missed Justice so much. She layed her head on the steering wheel and wailed like a baby.

"That bitch Skye, took my husband away from me and she's gonna pay. My plan to use Kareem to get him to talk is working and I'm even enjoying my young boy toy while plotting my revenge," she said, pulling herself together.

-

Chapter Sixteen

Skye headed upstairs to put all the bags of clothes she'd just purchased in her room with a huge smile on her face. Being back in the Louis Vuitton and Neiman Marcus stores in Bal Harbour gave her a feeling she couldn't explain. The fact that she didn't have to look at prices or worry about getting beat up by Sandino because she'd spend too much made the experience even more enjoyable. She even made a special trip to Dulce, a shoe boutique owned by *Basketball Wives* star, Evelyn Lozada and purchased five pairs of top designer shoes.

Once inside her room, Skye glanced at all the different shoe boxes and displayed a huge grin. She'd always been a shoe hoe, and the sight of each designer's name only reconfirmed her obsession. She immediately sat down on her bed and pulled a pair out of the box and tried them on. After buckling the tiny strap on the Francesco Sacco sandals, she stood in the mirror admiring how good they looked on her freshly pedicured feet.

"Now these are hot," she said to herself.

When Skye looked over at the two pairs of Alexander McQueen shoes she'd also purchased, her smile became even larger. She held the black leather, six inch pump in the air, realizing it was love at first sight.

Jackie D.

"I can't wait to wear these, too."

After spending several minutes in shoe heaven, she reached in her purse and pulled out the stack of bills she'd withdrawn from one of Sandino's accounts and stashed them in her new safe that was hidden in the closet. Even though she really enjoyed all the splurging on herself, Skye's main goal was to stash away as much money as she could for the next rainy day. She refused to be broke again and was preparing for the future which didn't include living in that house under those circumstances forever.

"Tomorrow, I will hit the stores again bright and early. Shit...I have to do something to take my mind off being back in the house with that devil," Skye said as she closed her safe and covered it up with some clothes.

Skye had basically avoided Sandino for the past few days and got pissed off every time Quinn would come and ask her to assist him. She also noticed that Jordan had been avoiding his father as well.

She had a flash back remembering when Jordan busted in the door from school on Sandino's first day home from the rehab center. He was so excited about his first day of football practice but his mood quickly changed once he saw his father.

Sandino however, was glad to see Jordan and glad to hear that he was following in his footsteps playing football. When he saw Jordan's reaction to seeing him and the way he ran out of the room, Sandino lowered his head with a sad look on his face.

Skye knew his appearance was overwhelming for him, not to mention she knew both her sons had a lot of mixed emotions still bottled up inside when it came to their father. The only thing Skye regretted the most about leaving Sandino was the impact it had on them. She headed to the kitchen and opened the refrigerator. She stood poking around inside and pulled out a turkey and cheese sandwich she'd made earlier and a Pepsi. She popped the top instantly turning it up.

"Aahhhhh, now that's what I needed," Skye said, plopping down at the huge maple leaf granite bar in the kitchen. While sitting there, it reminded her of Ms. Petra and how she would come in the kitchen and sit at that very bar and talk with her almost every day while she cooked delicious Jamaican meals. Skye took a deep breath thinking about how much she missed Ms. Petra, and wondered how she was doing since Skye hadn't been able to locate her. She'd called the number Ms. Petra had given her only to find out the number had been disconnected.

"Ms. Petra, I really wish you were here to help me deal with this bullshit right now," Skye said, as a tear rolled down her left cheek. She quickly grabbed a napkin off the counter and wiped her face.

Weakness is no longer tolerated. I need to pull myself together. I'm the one in charge here, she thought.

Suddenly her thoughts were broken when Quinn walked into the kitchen. Her eyebrows lifted when she noticed he wasn't wearing his normal uniform. Instead he had on just a wife beater that exposed his ripped muscles and a pair of basketball shorts. Skye almost lost it when she saw the print in front of the shorts.

What the fuck? This dude is hung like a damn horse, she thought to herself.

"Thank you so much for watching Payton while I was gone. Since Jordan is out and I haven't had time to interview for a nanny, I really appreciate that. I do realize that's not a part of your job description."

"No problem. She actually went to sleep once I fed her, and has been asleep ever since, so I didn't mind," Quinn responded. "She's a good baby."

"Yeah, I lucked up with her."

"I know you're not drinking that garbage, Skye," Quinn said, frowning up his face up at the Pepsi sitting on the counter.

Jackie D.

"Yes, I am drinking it. You so called healthy people kill me, always talking about this isn't good for you, that isn't good for you. Shit, we're all gonna die anyway so why not go out enjoying something you like," Skye joked.

Quinn shook his head at Skye's comment. "I see right now I'm gonna have to get some healthy food up in here and get you on a good diet. Plus, how are you gonna keep that body tight if you keep putting junk in it?"

Skye blushed. "I guess you're right. I do need to start eating healthy, but at least I've started working out again. Shoot, you should've seen me a few months ago. I gained so much weight. But in all the right places though."

Quinn looked her up and down with a devilish grin. "I'm sure you did."

The two were quiet for a minute.

"Skye, I have to run out for a little while and I need you to go and sit with Sandino. He's already dressed and in his wheelchair. You can push him around outside for awhile if you want."

"Oh nooooo, I got something to do," Skye lied.

Quinn wondered why she was always purposely avoiding her husband. In fact he noticed that her son was doing the same thing

"Look Skye, technically it's my day off. I haven't been out of this house since I got here. I have to run and get a few personal things, but it will not take long."

Quinn hoped she didn't get upset for him speaking his mind or even worse fire him because he really needed the job. But he felt the need to challenge her because the more she avoided Sandino the harder it was going to be for her to deal with his condition. He turned to walk away then suddenly remembered he forgot to tell her she had a visitor while she was out.

"Oh yeah, a man stopped by while you were out earlier. His name was Bruze...Cruze or something like that. He said

144

he would come back a little later."

Skye's expression changed. She'd already told Cruze over the phone that she needed some time and he wasn't respecting her wishes.

Quinn noticed how upset she got. "Is everything alright? I assume that wasn't somebody you wanted to see."

"You assumed right, but thanks for the message," Skye responded.

After leaving the kitchen, Quinn reappeared a few minutes later. He pushed Sandino into the kitchen. "Why don't you take him outside by the pool so he can get some sun?"

Skye gave Quinn the evil eye. "Who the hell works for whom around here?"

Quinn threw up his hands. "Just an idea," he said, walking out of the door.

Finally deciding to take Quinn's advice, Skye grabbed her Pepsi along with some other items. She paused when her stomach started to growl and decided to take a few bites of her sandwich. When she looked over at Sandino starring at her, she became irritated.

"Can I enjoy my damn food without you drooling at it?" she spat. "You're about to make me lose my appetite." When he kept looking, Skye walked over to him. "Evidently your ass is hungry so here," she said, stuffing half of her sandwich into his mouth making him gag. Skye then pushed Sandino outside near the pool talking shit the entire time.

"When the hell did my name get RN, at the end of it? This is some bullshit. Quinn is pushing his luck with the stunt he just pulled."

Skye positioned Sandino by the pool then sat several feet away from him in a lounge chair. As she sat reading a book on her Kindle and enjoying the sunshine, she could feel Sandino watching her with those crazy eyes that once terrified her. She rolled hers and acted like he didn't even exist.

Suddenly, Skye heard her cell phone ring. She looked at

Jackie D.

the caller ID and saw that it was Cruze calling. Instead of ignoring it like she normally did, this time she decided to answer.

"Hello."

"Hey, baby," Cruze said.

"I'm not your baby, and let's get something straight right now. Don't just be dropping by my house unannounced. I told you I needed some time so give it me," she said, slamming the phone down.

A few seconds later the phone rang again. Pissed, she looked at the caller ID again. This time is was Toni, Sandino's lawyer. Skye debated on whether or not to answer. She was enjoying her day and wasn't in the mood to deal with any business, so Skye decided to let the call go to voicemail and listen to her message later.

When she saw Sandino looking at her again like he was wondering who was calling, Skye frowned up her face at him. "Why the hell are you looking over here? You need to mind your damn business and don't be worried about whose calling my phone." She then busted out laughing. "That's the same shit you use to tell me…wow!"

When Skye saw Toni calling a second time, curiosity took over. Once the phone stopped ringing, she quickly decided to check her voicemail.

Hi, Skye. This is Toni Vaughn calling. Hey listen, I'm calling to see if you've looked at the news lately. I'm pretty sure you have since this has been all over the local news as well as some of those entertainment shows. We really need to discuss the recent pictures that were surfaced displaying Sandino in his wheelchair. I do realize that you wouldn't have taken any pictures of him and submitted them to anyone, but it looks like someone else did. It also looks like it's now been brought to the world's attention that Sandino has been petitioned to take a paternity test. Now, of course you and I both know who is probably responsible for all this, and because

146

Jackie D.

Sandino doesn't need this negative publicity right now, I need for him to go ahead and be tested so we can clear things up. We can talk details when you call me back. Talk to you soon.

Skye cringed at the mention of the paternity test. Even though she hadn't bothered to watch the news, she already knew Asia was behind this shit one hundred percent. She immediately slammed the phone down and jumped up, walking over toward Sandino's face.

"That was your lawyer on the phone. She wants to move forward with the paternity test. I hope you're happy now. That bitch Asia is trying to take all your money, the little bit you will have left once I'm done spending it all. That's what you get for fucking that gold digging ass bitch!" Skye got behind the wheelchair and pushed it closer to the pool. "I should push your ass in the water and leave," she said, rolling him back and forth to the edge.

At that moment, Skye heard thunder and felt small rain drops start to fall. She went over and gathered her things.

"Since you always loved the rain, I'll leave you out here to enjoy it," she said, walking inside just as it started to pour down raining.

Moments later, Skye headed up to her newly furnished bedroom, glanced out the upstairs window at Sandino outside and thought, *maybe the rain will wash away all the dirt you did, bastard!*

When she approached Payton's room and peeked inside to confirm that she was still asleep, Skye headed back across the hall to her bedroom. Once inside she flicked on the ceiling fan and fell back onto her King sized platform bed. Her mind drifted to Cruze. It was obvious that he wasn't going to give her up without a fight. With him constantly blowing up her cell phone and even stopping by the house now, Skye had to make a decision whether it was really over between them.

For once, she was enjoying her life without a man. Being single and being in charge of her own life was some-

147

Jackie D.

thing she'd never experienced and it actually felt good. But as much as she tried to occupy her mind, Skye couldn't help the fact that she did miss Cruze. The way he was so nurturing to her needs always made her feel so special. Not to mention the sex between them was off the chain.

Actually just thinking about it made her hot. As soon as the thought of his dick entered her mind, Skye reached inside her jeans and started playing with her pussy. She was horny as hell and needed to relieve some stress. For some reason, her mind suddenly shifted from Cruze and she started fantasizing about Quinn. Deciding to pleasure herself before Payton woke up, she went to her closet and retrieved the nine inch Rabbit Pearl vibrator she'd just purchased. With five speeds, Skye read on the box that it was suppose to send a woman into complete ecstasy, and she had every intention on finding out.

"We'll see about that," Skye said, removing the vibrator from the box and cleaning it off.

After putting lubrication on it, she removed her pants and laid back on the bed opening her legs wide. She slid the vibrator inside and hit the first speed. With her head tilted back, a chill ran through her body as she moaned and squeezed one of her breasts.

"Oh my God, this feels so good," she whispered. Deciding to take it up another notch, Skye hit another speed. She gasped for air and tried to refrain from moaning so loud.

"Oh, oh oh," Skye mumbled in complete pleasure as she grinded the vibrator as if it was a dick. Her body started jerking when she took it up to another speed.

"Oh shit...oh shit."

Her self pleasing was suddenly interrupted when she heard Jordan yelling out her name. He then started banging on her door.

"Mom, please come downstairs something is wrong!" he demanded.

When did he get home, Skye wondered as she turned

the vibrator off, pulled it out of her and jumped off the bed. She slid her new toy under her pillow before pulling up her pants and running out of the room. Worried that something might have happened to Payton she ran downstairs towards Jordan's voice.

"Ma, I saw him outside in the rain and pulled him inside, that's when he started shaking. Ma, do something!" Jordan yelled while leaning over Sandino's chair.

As she watched Sandino having convulsions and his eyes rolling back in his head, Skye shrugged her shoulders.

"Well, what you want me to do about it? I thought something was wrong with Payton," Skye replied unenthused.

"Mom, what's wrong with you?" Jordan yelled, as tears started to build up in his eyes. All of a sudden Quinn walked into the house and ran over.

"Move back Jordan, he's having another seizure."

Quinn pulled Sandino out of the chair onto the floor cushioning his head then rolling him onto his side to prevent him from choking on his fluids or vomit.

"Why are his clothes soaking wet?" Quinn asked.

Neither Jordan nor Skye answered him.

Quinn monitored Sandino as the seizure lasted about three minutes, after which Quinn started talking to Sandino.

"Are you okay, Sandino? Wink your eye once for yes twice for no."

When Sandino winked once, Quinn and Jordan picked him up and placed him back in the chair before Quinn pushed him to his room.

Jordan stood looking at Skye.

"Ma, I know my dad hurt you really bad, but he is still a human being. I don't know you anymore. All you do is shop. You never spend time with us like you used to. Have you even called to check on Kareem?" Jordan didn't even wait for her response before he walked away shaking his head.

Even though Skye felt bad that Jordan felt that way, she

Jackie D.

still could care less about Sandino. In her mind, he deserved much worse.

Chapter Seventeen

Kareem laid on the couch at Felicia's house pouting, still pissed off about seeing a man leaving her house two days before. Although Felicia told him it was her cousin, he still felt she wasn't being completely honest with him. He grabbed his Playstation controller and started a game of NBA 2K12 to take his mind off the possibility that Felicia might be cheating on him.

Several minutes later, Felicia walked into the house struggling as she carried groceries. Kareem was so involved in the game he didn't hear her come in. She slammed the food down on the counter pissed when she saw the trashcan overflowing and dirty dishes piled up in the sink. When she glanced in the living room and saw Kareem still lounging on her Italian leather sectional and stuff thrown throughout, she instantly got mad.

She'd never allowed anybody in her all white living room and now he was posted up in there with his game system attached to her 60' inch flat screen. She was beyond sick of Kareem being in her house and didn't know how much longer she could put up with him. He was totally disrespecting her once immaculate house.

Felicia liked to keep things a certain way and in the

short time he'd been staying there, Kareem didn't respect her prized possessions. Not to mention, Kareem was lazy, spoiled and very insecure. Felicia was used to having her space and living with him was like taking care of a child. At least when Dre stayed with her he cleaned up after himself. Being in prison had him on a structured routine and he cleaned the house actually better than she did.

"I want to kick his ass out so bad, but I have to deal with it a little while longer so I can work my magic on him a few more times and hopefully get some information," Felicia said to herself.

She had plans to cook him dinner and serve him some good sex for dessert, seducing him in ways he'd never imagined. After that, she would try and use reverse psychology to get him to open up over pillow talk.

Felicia walked into the living room and started picking up Kareem's things. She then started yelling after seeing his sneakers on her $4,000 hand-woven Persian rug.

"Look Kareem, this is not your mother's house. I told you before to use the family room to play your stupid ass game. You need to clean this shit up. I'm not your maid. And stop sitting around here pouting. How many times do I have to tell you the guy you saw was my cousin and he just stopped by to see me? I even offered to call him back over here and introduce you to him, but you declined so let the shit go," she said, stomping though the house. "And clean up your dishes and take the fucking trash out!" she yelled, slamming her bedroom door.

Kareem cut the game off and looked in the direction of Felicia's room. The last thing he wanted to do was upset her. He got up off the couch and started cleaning up the mess he'd made. He then unplugged his game system, took it along with his shoes and clothing into the spare bedroom. After making sure everything was perfect, Kareem headed to the kitchen and rinsed his dishes off before placing them into the dish washer.

After wiping down all her granite counter tops, he swept and mopped the kitchen floor, then took out the trash.

Kareem walked around surveying everything to make sure it was totally spotless before knocking on her bedroom door. When she didn't answer he turned the knob and walked inside. He saw a trail of clothing leading to the bathroom and heard the shower running as Mary J's new CD *My Life 2* blasted from her iPod touch. This instantly turned him on while he proceeded to the bathroom. The aroma of the vanilla honey exfoliating body wash she used lingered throughout and instantly invaded his nostrils. When he heard the water turn off, Kareem grabbed a towel and stood at the stained shower doors waiting for her.

When Felicia opened the doors, he admired her perfect body and the way she had her long weave pulled up with a large clamp. It was so sexy to him. When Felicia noticed him standing amongst the steam she was startled.

"Are you trying to give me a heart attack?" she asked, stepping out.

Kareem wrapped the oversized towel around her body. "I'm sorry, baby. I know I've been acting like an asshole and haven't been cleaning up behind myself. It's a bad habit because I had a housekeeper pick up my shit all my life, but I promise to do better. I really appreciate everything that you're doing for me. And yeah, a nigga has been a little insecure. But the thought of you..." He opened the towel and looked down at her naked body again. "The thought of somebody getting this beautiful body or you in general had me fucked up. Do you forgive me?" he asked, rubbing his hands up and down her back.

"I guess, Kareem. But you have to start trusting me and respecting my house."

"Okay, deal. Let's start over," he said, picking her up.

Felicia draped her arms around Kareem's shoulders as he carried her into the bedroom laying her on the bed. While

Kareem stood looking at her thinking how lucky he was to have her in his life. She began playing with her clit, giving him a mischievous grin as she slid her fingers inside her pussy. She bit down on her lip and opened her legs wider going in deeper with her fingers.

Kareem quickly starting removing his clothes as Mary J. continued to play in the background setting the mood even more. He leaped on the bed beside her, and pulled her close, smelling the vanilla scent on her body. He then kissed Felicia's lips, looking into her seductive eyes.

Felicia reached over and grabbed Kareem's throbbing dick and began rubbing it against her pussy driving him crazy.

"You want this wet pussy, baby?" she whispered in his ear in a sexy voice.

"Yes…please," he moaned giving her a deep passionate kiss trying to suck all the air from her lungs.

A few seconds later, she slid down and popped his dick in her mouth. Kareem let out a gasp as she began bobbing up and down on his dick. She made slurping sounds making sure to lick from the balls to the shaft and using her hand to jerk and squeeze his balls also. Kareem rolled his head back in pure ecstasy as she preformed with the best muscle control from her mouth he'd ever experienced.

"Damn, Le Le," he moaned out loud, grabbing her hair and thrusting in and out of her mouth.

Anxious and feeling himself about to cum, he pulled her up and got on top of her. Felicia gasped when he entered inside her. Kareem was very large for his age which really thrilled her. She let out a low scream as he pumped hard and fast. She returned the humps making sure she flexed her pussy muscles around his dick.

When she heard her husband's favorite song *Encore* by Jay- Z coming from her cell phone, she turned her head in the direction of her dresser. After hearing the ringtone chime over and over again, she knew it was Dre calling.

Kareem also heard her phone, but tried not let it spoil his mood and quickly took his mind back to the pussy when he felt Felicia's juices running down the shaft of his dick.

When she felt her clit tingling, she grabbed the back of Kareem's head as she exploded all over his dick. Kareem felt her legs trembling and it intensified his motions as he pounded and pounded until his body jerked and he released.

"This is the best pussy I've ever had," he blurted out while collapsing on the bed. They both laid naked and satisfied in each other's arms.

After several minutes passed, Felicia reached over and rubbed her hands through Kareem's curly hair.

"Kareem, can I ask you a question?" she mumbled in his ear.

Kareem looked over at her with lust filled eyes. "After what you just did to me Le Le, I'll tell you whatever you want to know."

Dre sat at his brother's desk at the shelter, pissed that Felicia wasn't picking up her phone. When he dialed it again and it went straight to voicemail, he decided to leave her a message.

"Felicia, I been callin' you all damn day. I hope you makin' some progress wit' that boy. Call me back," he said, slamming the phone down.

Dre had already been to the shelter several times searching for clues about Justice, but he decided to go back again just in case he'd missed something from before. Opening the blinds, he had a hard time looking around because the shelter no longer had electricity.

He started going through Justice's desk drawers and found a picture of Mercedes standing in front of the shelter for its grand opening. His heart dropped looking at her beautiful smile. Even though she'd done him wrong he would always love her and was devastated when he found out she was killed.

"I miss you, baby girl. You were and always will be the only woman I ever truly loved," he said, shaking his head.

He then started thumbing through the huge pile of mail that was stuffed in the overflowing mailbox outside. Most were past due bills along with several thank you cards from women who'd stayed at the shelter and managed to successfully move on. After Justice was officially reported as missing, the state of Georgia immediately relocated the remaining ladies to other shelters and stopped all financial payments. When Dre opened up a letter saying that Justice was behind on the mortgage for the building and they were threatening foreclosure, he shook his head thinking, *my brother was really in debt.*

Even though Dre missed his brother and wanted to find out what happened to him just as much as Felicia did, truth be told he wanted to take over the shelter; turning it into a gym with a boxing ring, punching bags and state of the art equipment. The only problem was he was broke and needed to collect on his brother's life insurance policy. Although he wasn't the beneficiary on his policy, Felicia promised to split the money with him if he helped her find out what happened to Justice. They'd already filed a missing persons report, and the police were investigating but without a body they had to wait seven years before they could collect on his policy. Time was ticking and Dre was getting extremely impatient waiting on Felicia to get information out of Kareem.

"Fuck this. It's time I take matters into my own hands."

Chapter Eighteen

Asia stood in line at the liquor store with a cheap bottle of Absolute Vodka tucked under one arm and the baby in the other. She'd been so stressed out it seemed as if the only thing that seemed to relax her lately was alcohol. After releasing the pictures of Sandino, the reporter had offered Asia a paid interview for her side of the story, but after she received a phone call from Sandino's lawyer threatening her with a cease and desist letter, Asia hadn't gone through with it. She did, however warn Toni that if Sandino didn't take the paternity test ASAP, she would continue to blast him in the media.

As Asia continued waiting, her patience was beginning to run thin as the clerk took his time ringing up the customer in front of her. She listened as the older white gentleman told the clerk he was new in town and was looking for something fun to do. He then went on to say, he preferred to go to a nice bar instead of a crowded night club. The clerk responded by telling him about some of the bars in the area.

"Hey, can we speed things up? You're holding up the line," Asia said, shifting her weight from one side to the other.

When the clerk and the customer continued to chit chat, Asia was pissed that she was being ignored. Deciding to walk to the front of the line, she was about to go off, but paused

Jackie D.

when she saw the attractive white man pull out a gold money clip full of hundred dollar bills and pay for his items. Asia's eyes instantly bulged out of her head and lit up like Times Square on New Year's Eve. Suddenly the lyrics from the old Wu-Tang song popped into her head.

"Cash rules everything around me C.R.E.A.M. get the money, dollar dollar bill y'all."

After watching him walk out, she quickly paid for her items, went to her truck to put the baby inside, then walked over to the man's hunter green Jaguar XF just as he was about to pull off. She knocked on the window and smiled. As soon as he rolled the window down, Asia noticed how he was layered with the trinkets that only rich men would wear...not real flashy but symbols that said he probably had money to blow. His solid gold Rolex shined like the sun as she glanced at it; knowing it wasn't a knockoff by the way the second hand swept the dial.

Only a pro can spot a real Roley, she thought to herself.

Wearing a low cut tunic dress, Asia could see him looking at her breasts as she leaned over on his door teasing him. This was all part of her plan to get him to notice her.

"Hello, I couldn't help but overhear you in the store saying that you were looking for something fun to do tonight."

The man looked down at her breasts again and licked his lips. "Yes, I did. Do you have something in mind?"

"Since I heard you say you prefer a bar vs. a night club, there's this really sexy restaurant called Nobu on Collins Avenue that you might enjoy. Their food is delicious and they make great Mango Martinis," Asia said, playing with her hair.

"Nobu sounds like my kind of place," he said, looking her up and down like she was a piece of meat.

"Let me give you my number and maybe I'll join you. I'm looking for some fun myself tonight." She batted her eyes.

Asia hadn't had a decent meal since arriving back in Miami, so she'd purposely chosen the place. After giving him her number she walked off making sure she did her famous stallion stride. As he watched her ass like a deer in head lights, she knew he would call her within the hour.

It's crazy how dirty old white men love black woman, but will never commit to one, she thought.

Nevertheless, Asia seemed to always attract rich white men even though technically she came onto him, and this one was no exception. After getting into her truck and pulling off, she started into traffic as thoughts continued to race through her head. She suddenly thought about the conversation she had with the lawyer's assistant about Skye and the renovations to their house. Suddenly, she made a u-turn in the middle of the street and headed over to Sandino's house again to see what was really going on. Asia opened the bottle of vodka and poured some in a cup while taking huge sips as she drove to Sandino's house on a mission.

"If that bitch Skye thinks I'm just gonna go away, she's wrong. Ain't that right, SJ?" she yelled to her son in the back seat as if she expected him to answer.

Asia turned up the music when she heard her favorite song, *Someone Like You* by Adele.

"I heard that you're settled down, that you found a girl and you're married now," she sang along.

She finished off the vodka in her cup and instead of pouring another one she just turned the bottle up. As she continued to listen to Adele she found herself unable to hold back the tears. Between the postpartum depression she'd diagnosed herself with and the amount of alcohol she consumed Asia was an emotional wreck.

When she reached Sandino's street, Asia drove by slow and parked across the street when she saw Jordan outside in the yard throwing his football in the air. Looking like a miniature Sandino, she couldn't believe how much he'd grown.

The yard had been cleaned up well and seemed back to normal. Asia even noticed a few freshly planted orchids. She continued to watch, wondering where Skye was until Asia saw her pull up in a white convertible Bentley Continental GT with thirty day tags a few minutes later. Asia fumed as Skye got out carrying several shopping bags from Saks, Hermes, and Tory Burch. She went ballistic and started punching the steering wheel immediately.

"No this bitch ain't driving a brand new fucking car! The car that I want! These muthafuckas are really trying to play me. I can't even get a dime, but this bitch is flossing around town."

When Asia saw Skye and Jordan go inside, she quickly grabbed her pocket knife out of the glove compartment and jumped out of the truck. "Let's see how much you floss now, bitch," she said, while running toward the driveway.

Looking around to see if anyone was watching, Asia displayed a revengeful grin right before driving the blade deep into the front passenger tire. She then made her way around the entire car until the other three tires had also been destroyed.

"This will teach her ass not to fuck with me," Asia said before looking around again.

Knowing she wasn't done, Asia climbed up onto the hood never bothering to remove her shoes before quickly pulling up her dress. Asia didn't have to worry about the alarm since Skye hadn't activated it, but she had to act fast before someone drove by. Pulling down her panties, Asia squatted in the perfect position then proceeded to piss all over the hood of the brand new car. The more she thought about Skye living the lavish lifestyle she wanted, Asia didn't care who saw her at that point as she looked up at the living room window. To her surprise, someone was watching her all along. Asia started at the man as he looked at her with complete shock. But instead of stopping, she flashed a devious smile.

After leaving a puddle of urine, she jumped down and ran back to her truck.

Jackie D.

"I hope you like the gift ,bitch! I'll be backkk," Asia said in her terminator voice before skidding off.

She cursed and continuously banged the steering wheel with her fist while making her way out of the neighborhood. The moment she thought about Skye not locking the door, Asia considering turning around and leaving a bowel movement in the driver's seat until her phone vibrated. Realizing it was a text, she finally decreased her speed, and read the message. It was from the guy at the liquor store, inviting her to a hotel for drinks later that night. A smile finally consumed her face.

I would loooove to. Meet you there at 8, she texted back.

Guess instead of eating some food he would rather get straight to the point and eat this pussy, she thought.

Later that night, Asia stood in the mirror piling foundation on her face. She then stepped back and admired herself in a tight fitting strapless dress that outlined every curve. It was as if the designer made the garment especially for her body.

"Damn, I look good," she said, blowing herself a kiss in the mirror.

Asia made sure she fed the baby more than usual so he could be extra full. She also made sure he was dry and asleep on the bed before leaving him alone. Asia figured since she'd done it before and everything worked out, there was nothing wrong with leaving him again, especially since she planned to be back within three hours. Moments later, she eased out of the room and left for her date with one thing in mind, getting some much needed cash.

Asia looked at the address he'd texted her earlier and realized it was only a few blocks away. A few minutes later she pulled up in front of the Hilton Bentley Hotel. With a motive on her mind, she decided it wasn't a good idea to valet park

Jackie D.

just in case she had to leave in a hurry. So, she found a parking space on the street and went inside before getting on the elevator and heading to the sixth floor.

Her feet were already starting to hurt in the five inch stilettos she wore. She wanted to reach down and pull them off so badly, but the thought of showing up with bare feet wasn't a good look. Most women would've been nervous about going to a strange man's hotel room, especially after being raped, but Asia was desperate and had her pocket knife in her purse for protection.

When the elevator door opened she made her way toward room number 624, then knocked on the door. He opened it immediately. His eyes were glued to her as Asia stood in front of him with a seductive stance. He was impeccably dressed in a short sleeve linen shirt with pants to match. Appearing to be at least sixty, he was a tall, solidly built man with silver colored hair and piercing blue eyes.

"You look so hot," he said, taking Asia by the hand and escorting her inside.

She immediately noticed the dim and romantic lighting in the hotel room as he walked over to the mini bar and opened a bottle of Veuve Clicquot. Asia watched him closely while he poured her a glass to make sure he didn't slip anything inside her drink. He then passed her a glass and held up his.

"Let's toast to a great evening."

"To a great evening," Asia repeated.

While sipping her drink she looked around admiring the nice, spacious ocean view suite. The eggshell colored room had a large, king size bed, a leather sofa and the highest quality of furnishings. She also noticed packets of condoms and lube on the table.

Checking her watch, Asia knew she didn't have much time to socialize. So, she finished off her drink and walked up to him, grabbing his dick. He looked at her with a devilish grin.

Jackie D.

"I see you're a woman who doesn't like to waste time. I like that," he said, removing his clothes.

Asia did the same.

Moments later, she got into bed and watched as he walked over to the condoms and opened a pack. *For an old white man, his dick is not that small*, she thought.

After putting on the protection, he quickly eased on top of her. He then slid his fingers inside her pussy and started sucking and licking on her breasts at the same time.

"Ummm, that feels good," Asia moaned.

Unable to wait, he slid inside her. He moved his dick in and out teasing her wet pussy, which drove him crazy. Asia started grinding him extra hard pulling out all of her best moves. He started growling like a grizzly bear and pumping her extra fast. He grabbed her tight and pounded her pussy rough and hard to the point where it was beginning to hurt. At that moment, she suddenly had a flash back of Zoe raping her. Asia was just about to start fighting him off until she heard him grunting loudly and yelled he was about to explode. Within seconds, it was all over. He came so hard he looked down hoping the force of his semen didn't destroy the condom.

Asia looked over at the clock beside the bed and saw that he'd only lasted seven minutes. Under normal circumstances she would've been pissed, but this time she was actually grateful. With a gentle but powerful shove, she pushed him off of her. After a few gasps, the man was snoring.

Asia shook her head. "That's a damn shame," she said, grabbing her phone and taking pictures of him naked. She then included herself in a photo kissing him with her tongue out. When he almost woke up, she quickly layed back down and pretended to be asleep. The minute he started snoring again, she eased up and went for his pockets. Asia took the entire $800 dollars he had along with his American Express card.

"This was like taking candy from a baby," she said,

quickly getting dressed and slipping out his hotel room a few minutes later. After safely getting away, she checked her watch and smiled from ear to ear. "It only took me less than an hour to accomplish my goal."

Feeling extremely proud, she whipped out her phone and sent the man she'd just robbed a text message.

Thanks for the money & your credit card. If u call the police or report this card stolen I will send pictures of our wild night to your wife on the address I got off your license. I would hate to break up your marriage Mr. James Randolph!

Asia smirked as she hit send.

With some money, a credit card and a plate of food that she'd picked up, Asia walked up to her hotel room feeling on top of the world. Approaching her room, she was extremely surprised that the baby was still asleep and not crying to the top of his lungs.

"He's being trained well," she said to herself.

After putting her hotel card in the door, and walking inside, Asia immediately dropped her food on the floor and gasped when she looked over toward the bed. The baby was gone!

Chapter Nineteen

"Oh my God... where the hell is my son?" Asia yelled out.

She frantically ran around her hotel room looking on the floor, in the closet, and in the bathroom for her baby. When she realized he wasn't in the room, Asia sat on the bed to try and gather her thoughts. She couldn't even think straight. She picked up the hotel phone but quickly hung it up.

"I need to call 911... but then they will know that I left him in the room alone or worse, think I did something to him. Think Asia... think. Maybe I left him in the truck," she said in her delusional state of mind.

She took off running out of the room, through one of the exit doors and ran down the steps to the parking lot. After reaching her truck, she desperately tried to open the back door, but it was locked.

"Damn it... I left my fucking keys." Asia put her hands up against the window and peeked inside, but the baby wasn't there. Feeling like she was about to lose her mind, she hit the hood of her truck.

"What have I done?" she asked herself. As bad as Asia didn't want to alert anyone about what was going on, her gut feeling told her something was wrong. She ran back inside the hotel lobby for assistance. "Please help me, my baby has been kidnapped. Lock the hotel down!" Asia yelled out of breath.

The clerk working at the front desk looked at Asia strange before she picked up the phone and made a quick call. She then came from behind the desk to try and calm her down.

"Ma'am, the police have been called. Please take a seat and try to calm yourself down," the clerk suggested.

"Bitch, are you serious? My baby is missing! What the hell do you mean take a seat and calm down?" Asia snapped.

The clerk stepped back insulted, then walked away and headed back to her desk mumbling something under her breath.

Asia covered her face in frustration. A few seconds later she started pacing back and forth and talking to herself. "I have to find my baby. He's the only way I'll be able to get my money from Sandino," she muttered to herself walking around the corner trying to get herself together.

Asia was sweating profusely from all the alcohol and felt like she was about to pass out when all of a sudden she caught a glimpse of a suspicious looking man with a black hooded sweatshirt on walking across the courtyard. Asia watched as he made his way across the grass and into a door on the other side of the hotel. Catching a second wind, she took off running after him thinking he might have something to do with SJ's disappearance. But after reaching the other side of the hotel, the man was no longer in sight. Irritated that she'd lost him, Asia's body froze when she heard a baby crying. She immediately started banging on all the hotel doors that were nearby.

"That's my baby! He took my baby!" she screamed.

No one came out of the first two doors she banged on, but by the time she reached the third, the hooded man opened with ease. Asia went crazy and started fighting him, trying to push her way inside his room.

"Where's my baby?"

He took off his hood and pushed Asia back trying to

calm her down. "Miss, I don't know what you're talking about. I just came back in my room from working out at the gym. There's no baby in here," he tried to explain.

"I don't believe you. I need to see inside your room, now!" Asia demanded.

Suddenly, a security guard walked up while Asia was trying to force her way inside the man's room once again. The guard immediately grabbed her arm, pulling her away.

"I'm so sorry for the disturbance, Mr. Brewington. Everything is under control now," the guard assured.

"Thanks, Steve. I really hope you can help this young lady find her baby," he said before closing his door.

"Get your hands off me! You need to check inside his room!" Asia yelled, pulling away from the guard.

"Look, Miss, your baby isn't in his room. Let's go!"

"I'm not going any damn where!"

The guard backed away and fanned his nose after smelling the vodka on her breath.He was really becoming impatient. "We can either do this the easy way or we can do this the hard way. I can't have you disturbing the other guests in this hotel," he stated with a stern look.

"Ain't nobody scared of your fake rent-a-cop ass. Somebody took my baby and you're treating me like I'm the criminal."

Instead of responding, the guard shook his head in disbelief, escorting her down the hall. When Asia passed a woman standing in her room's doorway with a crying baby in her arms, she realized that it wasn't her son she heard after all.

"Why are you holding me so tight? I made an honest mistake. I thought that man had my baby. Who was he anyway? You act like he was the President of the United States," Asia said, trying to pull away from his tight grip.

The security guard continued to forcefully hold Asia as he escorted her to the lobby.

"He's one of the contractor's working on the renovations for the hotel, if you must know."

"Look, this is getting out of hand. I just wanna find my baby, that's all."

When they reached the lobby, Asia saw the front desk clerk talking to two Spanish looking police officers. At that moment, she pulled away from the guard and ran over to them.

"Thank God, you finally got here. Somebody kidnapped my son. I only left him for a few minutes to get something out my truck and when I came back to my room the door was open and he was gone. I tried to tell that stupid ass security guard the same thing, but all he wants to do is fucking harass me. We need to lock down the hotel and go door to door!" Asia ranted.

One of police officers reached for his handcuffs and grabbed Asia pulling her hands behind her back.

"You have the right to remain silent. If you choose to give up your right to remain silent, anything you say can and will be used against you in a court of law..."

Asia's eyes widened. "What the hell are you talking about? Get the hell off me! Why are arresting me? You should be out there looking for the person who kidnapped my son!"

"Your son wasn't kidnapped, Ms. Jones. He's been placed in the custody of Child Protective Services, and you're being arrested for child abandonment."

"What? I only left him for a second to go to my truck!" Asia fired back.

"We saw you leave on the hotel surveillance camera hours ago, Ms. Jones. Meanwhile, a guest called the front desk after hearing your son crying at the top of his little lungs for hours. When the desk clerk sent security to your room, the baby was all alone."

"That's a lie!" Asia wailed.

The officer shook his head. "I seriously doubt that. From what I can smell, it seems like you might've been out drinking."

"We've been waiting for you to return," the other officer chimed in.

Asia looked at the clerk realizing that she knew all along. The police even knew her name which meant, the clerk had already given them her information. "Why didn't you tell me you knew where my baby was, bitch! You set me up!"

"Come on, Ms. Jones," one officer said.

"Get off me! I have a son by a famous football player. You're going to be sorry for this shit once his lawyer finishes with you. I'm going to sue you and this hotel!" Asia blasted. As the officers proceeded to escort her out of the lobby, Asia's dress was now pulled up around her waist exposing her panties. "Can you at least pull my fucking dress down?"

The woman who'd called security after hearing the baby crying was standing outside smoking a cigarette when Asia and the police walked past her. She started shaking her head.

"That poor little baby, he didn't ask to be brought in this world. You should be ashamed at yourself!" the lady preached.

Asia looked over at her with an evil stare. "Shut the hell up old lady," she responded as they placed her into the waiting police car.

LIFE *After* A BALLA

Chapter Twenty

After a nap, Kareem awoke to find the afternoon sun filtering through the wood blinds in Felicia's family room. He stretched and sat on the couch irritated that he hadn't heard from his mother in days. He knew she was probably still upset about his decision not to move back to Miami with them, but living with his father again was out of the question. His father was dead. Regardless of the fact that he'd survived a gunshot wound, in Kareem's mind Sandino no longer existed and he had every intention on keeping it that way.

I guess me and my mother don't understand each other, he thought. *I don't understand how she could go back and live with the nigga who beat her ass every day and she doesn't understand why I want to be with Le Le.*

Skye had made it absolutely clear that she would never accept his girl as part of their family so now Kareem considered Georgia to be his home. *Besides, Le Le got me so open I'm even thinking about asking her to marry me after I find a job.* Kareem smiled. *Le Le's ass so high maintenance though the ring would probably set a nigga back big time.*

At that moment, Kareem wondered where she was. Just before he'd fallen asleep he remembered her telling him she was going to clean up, but since he didn't hear the Frankie

Jackie D.

Beverly and Maze greatest hits CD she normally played while cleaning, Kareem didn't know what was going on.

"Le Le!" he called out. "Le Le!"

When she didn't answer, Kareem jumped up and ran over to the window. After seeing her car in the driveway, he figured she could only be one or two places. He'd only lived with her for a little over a month and already knew her routine. When Felicia was at home, all she wanted Kareem to do was keep the house clean and fuck her on a regular basis which she was pretty boisterous about. When she was quiet, Le Le was normally in her spa-like bathroom or her precious walk-in closet, and Kareem wasn't allowed to disturb her.

Walking back to the couch, Kareem reached for the remote so he could change the channel. When it wasn't on the table he searched between the cushions, but still couldn't find it. Getting down on his knees, he reached underneath the couch hoping the remote would turn up there. However when he felt something and pulled the object out, Kareem was shocked to find a man's basketball shoe.

"What the fuck? Whose shoe is this?" he asked looking inside. "And it's a size thirteen. This shit don't belong to me." Instantly, all kinds of crazy thoughts started going through his mind. "This shoe probably belongs to the nigga I saw leaving that day. Now that I think about it, Le Le has been acting different every since I moved in with her. I guess I'm in the way... fucking up her groove."

Beyond pissed, Kareem stood up and threw the shoe across the room. But instead of confronting her he decided to look around the house to see if he could find anything else that belonged to the mystery man. His first stop was going to be the bedroom located at the end of the hall that Felicia always kept locked. She'd told him on numerous occasions that she kept the room locked because there was tons of junk inside from her old business and she wasn't ready to clean it. Up until now, Kareem didn't care to question her outlandish reason, but now

172

he realized the explanation didn't make sense.

Kareem went into the kitchen and grabbed a knife out of the drawer, then headed upstairs to the suspicious bedroom. With just a little bit of tampering with the doorknob, he managed to break the lock and was inside within seconds. Looking around he quickly realized that she'd lied to him. Just like the rest of the house, the room was completely spotless.

"Why the hell did Le Le tell me this room was packed with junk? What is this bitch hiding?" Kareem walked over and opened the closet door. When he saw several pairs of men's shoes on the floor along with clothing neatly hanging in the closet, he went ballistic. "What the fuck is going on around here?"

Puzzled and angry, Kareem left but continued to search, marching straight to Felicia's bedroom. Hearing the water coming from the bathroom confirmed her location which gave him ample time to snoop. After searching under the bed for a few minutes and coming up empty, he suddenly thought about Felicia's sacred closet. Knowing that door was locked as well, Kareem performed the same bootleg locksmith job and made his way inside. He didn't see anything suspicious at first until he slid a long white coat to the side and noticed a large cardboard box. Curious to see what was inside, Kareem didn't waste anytime opening it up. Again, he didn't think much of it after seeing a lot of paperwork, several books and a few photos. However, when he came across a piece of paper with *Breaking the Cycle Women's Shelter* letterhead on it, his questioning kicked into high gear.

"What the hell is she doing with paper from the shelter we stayed at?" Kareem wondered.

Grabbing one of the pictures, he continued to flip through them until one with Felicia in a wedding gown, instantly caught his attention. His eyes instantly enlarged. Not only was Kareem unaware that Felicia was ever married, but the man standing beside her in a tuxedo was none other than

Jackie D.

Justice. His heart rate began to increase as he saw one picture after the other of the happy couple smiling. In each picture they seemed to be on some sort of vacation and obviously enjoying each other's company. When Kareem came across a picture of Justice and the same man he'd seen leaving her house the week prior, it didn't take long for him to finally start piecing everything together.

So, that was Justice's car the guy was driving. No wonder Le Le has been asking me so many fucking questions. She wants to know what happened. She's been setting me up this whole time!

It was at that moment when Kareem looked at the white coat he'd pushed away from before and noticed the words, *Dr. Felicia Mitchell M.D.* engraved on the top right corner. Everything was all a lie.

Rage consumed Kareem's body as he stormed out of her bedroom and towards the bathroom. Hearing his rapid footsteps, Felicia who was only acting as if she was in the shower immediately tried to end her phone call when he stormed inside. However, before she had a chance to react, Kareem quickly snatched her up by both arms.

"So, bitch you been playing me the entire time, huh? Did you think I wouldn't find out what you were up to or who that nigga was?"

Startled, Felicia looked into Kareem's crazed eyes. "Get off me! What the hell is wrong with you?"

Realizing that she never cared about him and it was all just a ploy to find her husband's killer made Kareem go even crazier. At that moment, he pushed Felicia so hard it sent her body flying to the bathroom floor. Seconds later, he jumped on top of her landing several massive blows across her face. It all happened so fast, Felicia couldn't do anything but put up her hands to try and block the constant punches.

"Why are you doing this to me?" she asked as blood trickled down her nose.

174

Jackie D.

Without responding, Kareem put both of his hands around her neck and started applying pressure. Unable to breathe, Felicia became hysterical and started gasping for air and grabbing at his hands.

"I can't believe I actually fell in love with your old ass. My mother was right about you!"

Just the thought of her betraying him caused Kareem to suddenly throw another punch. He then grabbed Felicia by the hair and pulled her badly beaten body over to the toilet.

"You shady bitch. Let's see if you like using people after this," Kareem said, lifting the seat with one hand while pushing her face inside the bowl with the other. Felicia desperately tried to keep from drowning, but she was no match against the strong hold he held on the back of her head.

"I should kill your ass for playing with my fucking emotions, Felicia Mitchell!'"

Hearing Kareem call her by her real name, Felicia finally realized he'd found out who she really was.

He continued to push her head back and forth in the toilet water until suddenly she heard a male voice say, "Get your fuckin' hands off her nigga before I kill yo' ass."

Kareem instantly released his grip and turned around looking into the barrel of a gun. Dre had rushed over after hearing the entire incident over the phone. It was him Felicia was talking to when Kareem stormed in the bathroom.

Felicia coughed and cried uncontrollably.

Dre reached down and helped Felicia off the floor. "Are you okay?" he asked, still pointing the gun at Kareem.

"No…I'm…not," she said, coughing in between words. "What…are we going to do now? He knows who we are."

"Don't worry about that. Just let me handle it. Here, hold this and keep it pointed on his ass," Dre said, passing Felicia his Glock 17.

I shoulda took over a long time ago instead of wastin' time waitin' on Felicia's ass to make somethin' happen, Dre

175

Jackie D.

thought. He walked over to Kareem and got in his face. "Instead of beatin' on woman why don't you fight a man," he said, pushing Kareem against the wall. "I guess you inherited beatin' on women from your bitch ass father. I should crack your fuckin' head open right now."

Kareem looked at Dre wondering how he knew his father. But more or less he didn't ever want to be like him.

"I was locked up wit' your father and now I see you're just as heartless as that nigga was," Dre continued.

"Man, fuck you and him!" Kareem yelled.

Dre took the gun from Felicia's hand and told her to leave.

"No, wait Dre, don't do anything stupid," Felicia cried.

"Felicia, I said leave!" Dre roared. "Now!"

As soon as she closed the bathroom door, Dre took the butt of the gun and pistol whipped Kareem across his face. Blood spattered everywhere and it wasn't long before Kareem broke down crying.

"Shut your bitch ass up!" Dre yelled. "Let me hear you talk shit now!"

"Please don't kill me. I'll do whatever you need me to do," Kareem responded.

"Now that's what I want to hear. Did you kill my brother, Justice?" When Kareem didn't respond, Dre got in his face again. "Muthafucka, I asked you a question. Did you kill my brother?"

"No, I didn't!"

"Well, I suggest you tell me what happened. What about your mother? I don't wanna have to hurt your family, but I will if I don't get the information I need," Dre informed.

"Leave my family out of this."

"Then start talkin'! Where is Justice? Is he dead?" As soon as Kareem nodded his head, Dre's excitement escalated. "Where is his body?"

"I don't know, but I know someone who does," Kareem

snitched.

"I knew it. I knew y'all muthafuckas were involved. Who killed him? Who got rid of his body?" Dre pointed the gun at Kareem again to show him he meant business.

"My mother's boyfriend. Cruze." Kareem felt bad, but throwing Cruze under the bus seemed like the right thing to do.

"Call that muthafucka right now. I need to see him," Dre responded. "I don't even wanna know how shit went down. I just wanna know where my brother is."

"But I don't have his number. I…" When Kareem saw the seriousness in Dre's face, he took the cell phone out of his pocket and quickly called his mother. He prayed she'd answer.

"Hey, Kareem," Skye said when she answered the call. She sounded so excited to hear from him.

"Hey, Ma. How are things going?" Kareem, on the other hand sounded nervous.

"I actually can't complain. I'm on my way to Payton's doctor. She's recovering well and Jordan is doing great. How are you? We miss you."

"I miss you all, too. Hey Ma, is Cruze still in Georgia or did he come to Miami?"

"Can you believe he's in Miami now? Why?"

"Just wondering. Hey, I'm coming back to Miami. Things with Le Le didn't work out. I'll tell you about it when I see you," he informed her.

Skye smiled from ear to ear. Not only was Kareem moving back home, but it sounded like he was done with his girlfriend. *I knew it wouldn't last with that bitch.*

"Can you text me Cruze's number?"

"Yes, but why are you trying to reach Cruze? I thought you didn't like him."

Dre started waving the gun at Kareem telling him to cut his call short.

"I just need to talk to him about something, so text me

the number as soon as we hang up please."

"I hope you're not planning on doing anything illegal with him Kareem," Skye replied.

"No Ma, I just need to talk to him about something man to man. Since I don't have a father in my life Cruze is the closest thing to that right now."

"Yeah, alright. This still sounds a little fishy to me but I'll text you his number. I love you."

"I love you, too," Kareem said before ending the call. He tried his best to keep his voice from trembling.

While holding the gun on Kareem, Dre's mind drifted. *I wonder if the same person who killed Justice had something to do with Mercedes murder, too. It's just ironic that they died around the same time,* he thought.

When Kareem noticed Dre's blank expression, he decided to it was time to make his move. He dove over and rustled for the gun. When the gun suddenly went off, Felicia ran back into the bathroom.

"Oh my God!" she screamed.

Chapter Twenty One

Skye stood beside the table holding Payton's hand as she was examined by the chiropractor. Payton whimpered, clenching Skye as the doctor held her tiny little leg up in the air feeling around the bones.

"Its okay baby girl, he just wants to look at your leg to make sure it's all better," Skye said, trying to reassure her daughter. She could see in Payton's eyes that she was terrified and about to start screaming at any minute.

"I'm almost finished, Payton. You're being such a big girl," the doctor said in his thick Indian accent.

When Skye was able to get Payton to calm down, a few seconds later the exam was over. The doctor sat Payton up on the table, removed his rubber gloves, grabbed her file and wrote down some notes.

"Give this to the young lady at the desk on your way out. I need to see Payton back next week," he said, passing Skye a billing invoice. "Payton's first round of Physical therapy went well today. She's healing a lot faster than expected. This is remarkable progress being that she just got her cast removed two days ago. I hope she isn't afraid of water because her second round of therapy will be Aquatic. This type of therapy will reduce the stress placed on her joints while walking on her leg again. Also, this aspect of aquatic therapy is especially useful for healing fractured bones and increasing flexibility and strength back in her leg."

"Payton loves the water. She's been swimming since she was a baby. My kids had a personal swimming instructor for years," Skye informed him.

"That's great. Did they attend some type of program at the Miami city pool?" he questioned.

Skye immediately frowned and gave him the look of death. "City Pool? My kids have never been in a city swimming pool. I have a customized swimming pool at my Palm Island Estate. Thank you very much," Skye said, putting on Payton's shoes. She was pissed that the doctor had insulted her like she was some project chick.

"I didn't mean to offend you, Mrs. Washington. I just assumed that…"

Skye cut him off, "You just assumed that my kids were some o' poor black kids, huh? Well, sorry to disappoint you, but that's far from the case. And by the way I asked you once before not to call me *Mrs.* Washington," she said, picking up Payton and walking out of the room.

Skye was fuming as she approached the check out desk and handed Payton's form to the pale skinny receptionist.

"Okay, Mrs. Washington, I see that the Dr. Chopra would like me to schedule Payton's weekly physical therapy appointments for the remainder of the month. But I don't see where we have your insurance information on file."

"I can see none of you listen around here. You can call me Skye and no you aren't gonna be able to find it because the insurance I applied for is still in underwriting."

The receptionist looked up at Skye and turned up her nose then looked back at the computer screen.

"Well, today's visit has to be paid before I can set up anymore appointments."

"Not a problem. I'm going to pay with cash."

"Today's visit was $700.00," the receptionist informed. It was almost as if she expected Skye not to have the money.

Skye threw her brand new Balenciaga purse on the counter, reached inside and pulled out a stack of money. She peeled off some of the bills.

"Here's $4000.00. That should cover her bill for today and the next couple therapy sessions. Now schedule her appointments so I can get out of here and go shopping please," Skye said.

The receptionist looked at Skye once more before counting the money and passing her a receipt. It felt good to be able to pay her daughter's bill this time.

"What time do you prefer, morning or afternoon appointments, Mrs...I mean Skye?" Her entire attitude had changed.

"Mornings, please. I usually like to schedule my spa appointments in the afternoon," Skye said, rubbing her new found status in the woman's face.

The receptionist continued to look in the computer before printing off Payton's monthly schedule and handed it to Skye. "Thanks, we'll see you next week."

Skye gave her a fake smile and headed out the door. However, before they could leave the building she was surprised to see Cruze walking toward them.

"What are you doing here?" Skye asked.

Payton instantly lit up when she saw Cruze. She smiled and reached out for him.

He grabbed her from Skye's arms. "Hey, pretty girl, I missed you," he said, kissing Payton on the cheek. He looked at Skye. "I've missed you, too," Cruze uttered with a sad appearance.

Skye rolled her eyes and sucked her teeth. "How did you know where I was... are you stalking me?"

Cruze chuckled, "No, Jordan told me where you were. I was hoping to take you to lunch so we could talk."

I'm going to kill Jordan, she thought. "Hey, I just thought about something. Have you talked to Kareem? He called me about an hour ago and asked for your number."

"No, not at all. What did he wanna talk about?"

"I don't know, he wouldn't say." Skye rubbed the back of her neck where a brick of tension had suddenly formed.

"I'm not hungry and there's nothing to talk about."

As Cruze stared at her, their eyes locked. Skye could see the regret and knew that another apology was approaching.

"I'm sorry that I hurt you, Skye. You have no idea the pain I've felt over these past few weeks."

"Yeah, well you should've thought about that before you chose to lie," Skye countered.

"So, can you at least go to lunch with me? Haven't you been avoiding me long enough?"

Skye took a deep breath. "Look…I gotta go," she said, grabbing Payton and walking out of the door. She ignored Payton's cries as she continued to hold her arms out for him.

Cruze walked behind her checking out her new clothes, new designer purse and the diamonds blinging everywhere as they approached the lobby. When they walked outside and he saw Skye stroll over to her brand new Bentley, jealousy quickly consumed him.

Who am I kidding, I'll never be ever to compete with Sandino's money, he thought.

"Damn, you rolling like that now," he said, admiring the subtle twenty inch rims.

"Can you believe that bitch Asia slashed all four of my fucking tires the other day? She even pissed on it. Look." Skye pointed to a small dent on the hood. "That's from her standing on it. Now, I gotta get my shit fixed."

Cruze seemed shocked. "Pissed on it? Get the fuck outta here. How do you know it was her?"

"Because Sandino's nurse saw her from the window. By the time I knew what was going on, that bitch had left. He didn't know who the woman was, but who else would be crazy enough to do some shit like that? Asia better hope I don't run into her ass on the street."

"Maybe it was one of Sandino's other women," Cruze suggested.

"I seriously doubt it. Did you forget that Sandino is in a wheelchair? All the groupies have moved on. Ain't nobody thinking about his crippled ass anymore."

As they both laughed, Cruze grabbed Skye's arm and turned her body around to face him. "Can I please get a few hours of your valuable time?"

Skye laughed and shook her head. "Alright Cruze, follow me to Prime 112."

"Bet."

Cruze walked to his car hoping he would be able to get Skye to take him back this time. He was trying to give her some space, but he missed her like crazy and needed to make things right between them.

About fifteen minutes later, they pulled up at the restaurant. He observed as Skye got out of her new whip giving her keys to the valet. She had a different look about her; even the way she walked was different. She definitely had a slight arrogance about herself now.

"I have to admit though, she looks sexy as hell."

Skye was wearing a Rachel Roy knit tunic, a pair of jeggings and some sky high Christian Louboutin platform pumps. She certainly wasn't the same girl he'd been with in the past who constantly rocked oversized t-shirts and fake Ugg boots. Cruze even noticed the new confidence she had about herself, which was such a turn on.

I love the way her ass is sitting up in those pants. She definitely has lost some weight.

When Cruze got out of the car, he followed Skye and Payton into the restaurant. As they stood in the front area waiting for the hostess to return, Cruze stared at her the entire time but she purposely looked away in the other direction. When the hostess finally came back, he walked behind the desk and looked down at the list.

"Sorry for the delay. What's the name on your reservation?" he inquired.

"We don't have a reservation," Skye replied.

"Oh, well I'm sorry but we're only seating reserved guests at this time. The restaurant is packed because of a nearby convention," the hostess quickly informed.

Cruze became irritated. "Mannnn, let's get the fuck up outta here. They probably don't have shit Payton can eat anyway."

"You wanted to go to lunch, and this is where I wanna eat," Skye demanded. She reached inside her purse. "I know you can make an exception this one time," she said, slipping him a hundred dollar bill.

The man looked around before grabbing the money then took his crooked finger and skimmed down the list again.

"Oh yes, I see your name right here. Follow me this way," he said, escorting them to a table.

"Would you like a booster seat for the little one?" he asked.

"Yes, thank you," Skye replied.

Cruze continued to observe Skye. She slung her hair from side to side as they were being seated. Then when the hostess came back, he watched as Skye pulled out more money and passed it to him.

Cruze waited for the man to leave. "Damn, Skye how much were you gonna give the muthafucka? That's his damn job to get the seat. I can understand giving him some money for letting us up in here without a reservation. But the other money wasn't necessary."

"Look Cruze, do I tell you what to do with your money?"

Cruze shook his head. "No, but it's not your…" he

paused.

"Then what gives you the right to try and tell me what to do with my damn money? And yes, I said *my* money!"

Skye's new cocky attitude was starting to piss Cruze off. He held his composure as the waiter walked up.

"Hello, welcome to Prime 112. What can I get you all to drink?"

"A Hennessey and coke for me," Cruze said.

"And a peach Ciroc and mango juice for me," Skye added

Cruze was shocked that she was drinking. He could never get her to take a drink with him before.

"Damn, you drinking now, walking around all fly...jeweled up with your red bottoms on. I see you love being back in Miami," he joked.

"I'm doing what I had to do for my family."

"So, how is your family? How's Sandino? I saw the pictures of him on the news and I hear he's gonna be a new dad."

Skye rolled her eyes. "I guess you're trying to be funny, huh? If you must know, I'm not even gonna get involved with that paternity test shit. Sandino was just swabbed for his DNA a few days ago, so who knows what the results will be. His trifling ass probably got even more women out there claiming to have his baby."

"Help me understand something. It's obvious that you've changed now that you have money again. And all that shit you have on is the type of things you deserve, so I get that. But what I don't get is why the hell you can't forgive me for trying to go out and make some real money to give you those things?"

Skye sat there for a minute before speaking. "You just don't get it do you?"

"Get what, Skye? I love you. I miss you and the kids. I want us back the way we used to be."

"Cruze, it will never be back to the way it used to be. You lied to me. The trust was broken. We vowed to always be honest to one another no matter what. But you fucked it up."

"I know I fucked up, but I promise I'll spend the rest of my life making it up to you if that's what you want. I've never loved anybody the way I love you."

Skye looked at him and gazed into his warm brown eyes searching for signs of bullshit. But all she saw was sincerity. She tossed the thought of forgiving him in her mind. She really did miss Cruze and wondered if she could get through the rest of her life without him. But Skye also made herself a promise that she would never be hurt by a man again.

Suddenly, Cruze reached over and kissed Skye on the cheek. Surprisingly, she didn't stop him.

I'm breaking her down, he thought.

When the waiter came over with their drinks, Cruze pulled away. "Thanks, but we need a few more minutes before we order," Cruze informed him. As soon as the waiter walked away, Cruze grabbed her hand. "So, baby can you please forgive me and allow us to move forward? I know you miss me."

While Skye sat there in silence, Cruze's phone began to ring. Thinking whoever it was would definitely have to wait, he ignored the call. Not even three seconds passed before it started ringing again.

"Don't you think you should get that?" Skye questioned. "It might be Kareem."

"Yeah, you're right," Cruze replied. But once he grabbed his phone and realized that he recognized the number, he put the phone away.

"Guess it wasn't Kareem, huh?" Skye questioned.

"Nah...nah it wasn't."

"So, who was it...your drug connect?" she replied with a smirk.

"Funny," was all Cruze said.

As Cruze phone rung yet a third time, suddenly disappointment washed over Skye's face. It was as if the thought of him lying to her all over again resurfaced.

"I can't do this," she said, pulling her hand back.

"So, you can put up with all that Sandino bullshit, but you won't give me another chance?"

Skye stood up from the table and grabbed Payton out of the booster seat. "I'm sick of giving chances!" she replied just before walking out.

LIFE *After* A BALLA

Chapter Twenty Two

"He didn't answer!"

"Well, dial the muthafuckin' number again!" Dre yelled at Kareem while pushing the gun deeper into the back of his head. "If you try that dumb shit again, the next shot will be in your head instead of the ceilin'."

"Alright," Kareem said while wiping the tears from his eyes. He constantly put on an act trying to be hard, but in reality he wasn't anything but a spoiled little rich boy.

He waited several minutes as the phone rang for the second time, then looked at Dre. He favored Justice so much it was scary. He turned his attention back to the phone when Cruze finally picked up.

"Who's this?"

"What up, Cruze? It's me...Kareem."

"Damn, Kareem what's going on? Your mother told me you asked for my number."

"Umm...yeah I really needed to holla at you. How is everything going?" Kareem tried his best not to sound alarmed.

"I'm trying to maintain. I miss your mom so bad though. I'm glad you called me. I want to apologize to you. You know the last thing I ever wanted to do was hurt you guys."

"Yeah, we all make mistakes. But you need to try and make this right things right with my mom because we miss you."

Cruze paused before speaking. Kareem's remark had sent up a red flag.

Kareem never wanted me around and now suddenly misses me? Something doesn't sound right, he thought.

"Cruze, I need to see you. I have something to talk to you about."

"What's wrong? Is it something that can be talked about over the phone?"

"No, I need to talk to you in person. It's really important though. I hear you're back in Miami."

"Yeah, I've been out here for a while now, trying to win your mom over."

Kareem looked at Dre to make sure he was listening. "So, you're back in Miami?"

Cruze hesitated for a second. "Kareem, what's up man? Is everything okay? I just answered that question."

"Everything's cool. So, where are you staying?"

Feeling like something wasn't right, Cruze decided not to tell Kareem his whereabouts just yet. "I'm floating around. Just call me when you wanna hook up."

"Okay, so you want me to call you?" Kareem mimicked.

"Why are you repeating everything I say? Is something wrong, Kareem?" Cruze asked once again.

"Yes, I'll call you back once I'm ready. Good talking to you," Kareem replied before the phone went dead.

Dre pushed Kareem out of the bathroom into the living room were Felicia was pacing the floor. She was pissed off that Dre had shot his gun into her expensive Solistone ceramic ceiling tile.

"Dre, I'm not so sure about all this now. I think we

should just let him go," she complained.

"Let him go? Go look in the mirror at your damn face, Felicia. If I hadn't rushed over here when I did that nigga woulda killed you! You crazy if you think I'm doin' all this shit for nothin'."

Kareem looked at Felicia hard and long. He really had no intention on hurting her like that. He was so hurt that she'd betrayed him, he ultimately lost it. At that moment, Kareem realized that he did have a lot of his father's ways instilled in him. The thought of being anything like Sandino made him feel terrible. When Felicia noticed the way Kareem was staring at her, she looked away. Dre also noticed.

"Is something wrong, nigga? You upset that she turned you out, huh? Did you fall in love? Well, it was all part of the plan to use your dumb ass so we could find out information. But if you ever put your hands on her again I swear I'll kill your ass." Dre punched Kareem in the face to let him know he meant business. "Felicia, go pack a bag we about to drive to Miami."

"Drive? Are you serious? Do you know how long that's going to take? Can't we fly?"

"We can't fly, this nigga might try to snitch or run. Plus, I can't carry my guns on the plane. We gotta drive and hopefully this shit will go smooth, if not we might be driving back with a dead body in the trunk."

Dre backed his brothers BMW into the garage and hit the remote waiting for the door to go down. He then got out of the car and entered the house through the garage. He walked into the room where Kareem was tied up to a chair.

"I'm about to untie your legs. If you try to run I swear to God I'll go shoot your mother right in the fuckin' head! Do you understand?"

Jackie D.

Kareem looked at Dre wishing he could kill him. "Yeah."

"If you cooperate I'll let your family live again," Dre told him.

Kareem wondered what he meant by he would let them live again. Dre must have read his mind because he began to answer his question.

"You see young blood, your father sent me here to Georgia to find y'all and take your mother out. At that time I wasn't up to killing nobody, but that was then. I got much more money on the line now. So I need to know where my brother's body is so I can collect on it," Dre explained.

Dre was so wrapped up with talking about money, he didn't hear Felicia when she walked into the room wearing a pair of Prada sunglasses, jeans, a cute top, six inch Giuseppe heals and rolling her designer luggage. Dre shook his head. It looked like she was going on vacation with her girls instead of on a mission looking for her husband's body. Felicia was the true definition of a Diva even with all the bruises she'd sustained from Kareem fists, she still looked like a runway model.

Kareem stood up when Dre released his legs even though his hands were still bound.

"Remember what I told you. Don't do anything stupid," Dre said, pushing Kareem through the house and towards the garage door. When Dre saw Felicia getting comfortable in the front passenger's seat of the car he stopped her. "What you doing Felicia? You have to drive so I can keep my eye on him."

Felicia looked at Dre like he was crazy. "Oh no no no. I know you don't expect me to drive. This shit was your idea, remember?"

"Well, would you rather sit and hold the gun on your lover boy?"

Felicia shook her head no once again. She wasn't touching that gun in fact this whole trip wasn't supposed to be part of the plan. She huffed and puffed before finally walking around to the driver's seat. Even though she felt Kareem staring at her when she passed him, she got into the car without looking at his face. Dre pushed Kareem into the passenger's seat and pulled down the visor so he could watch him through the mirror. He then climbed in the back. Felicia started the ignition and hit the garage remote.

"Make a move or try somethin', and I'll blow your ass away," Dre said as they pulled out.

Four hours into the drive, Dre could see Kareem eyeballing him through the mirror on the visor as he kept fidgeting around in the front seat.

"What the fuck do you keep movin' around for up there? We just pulled over so you could piss about a hour ago! That nigga up to somethin'. Yo' Felicia, pull the car over, I'm sick of this muthafucka!" Dre demanded.

Felicia wondered what he was up too and looked at him in the rear view mirror. "Why, what you getting ready to do, Dre?" she asked concerned.

"Just pull over!"

As soon as Felicia pulled the car onto the side of the highway, Dre told her to pop the trunk. She reached down and hit the switch, wondering what he was getting ready to do. Dre looked around to make sure no other cars were coming. When the coast was clear he got out then walked to the front of the car, snatching the passenger door open. He bent down and ripped a piece of duct tape off the roll in the front seat and put in on Kareem's mouth, pulling him out of the car.

"Let's go, nigga," Dre said, pushing him toward the back of the car. "Get your ass in the trunk." He wanted Kareem to hurry up before another car came by.

Kareem stood there looking at Dre like he wasn't getting inside. A few minutes later, he took off running trying to get back into the front seat. Felicia could see the frightened look on Kareem's face when he tried to get back inside. Suddenly, Dre grabbed the back of his shirt and slung him against the car, hitting him in the stomach with several vicious blows. Kareem fell to the ground in pain.

"Now, get your ass in that trunk before it gets worse."

"Why are you doing that?" Felicia yelled.

Ignoring her, Dre picked Kareem off the ground and rushed him to the back of the car again. This time Kareem got in. After Dre slammed the truck closed, he ran to the driver's side.

"Move over Felicia, I'll drive. We'll never get to Miami as slow as you're drivin'."

"Why did you hit him like that? Hasn't he been doing everything you asked him to? And why did you put him in the trunk? He can't ride back there. The carbon monoxide from the exhaust could kill him."

Dre gave her a snide look. "You act like you in love wit' the nigga or somethin'. He'll be alright for a few miles. Your biggest concern should be hopin' that we find out where Justice's body is so we can get that life insurance money. Fuck that nigga back there. He's a punk just like his father!"

Felicia didn't respond. She was pissed off that Dre seemed to be more concerned about getting the money than finding out what really happened to his brother.

"Now we have to figure out where we're going to stay once we get to Miami so Kareem won't be detected. It's not like we can get a hotel room," Dre carried on.

"We can stay in Hollywood, Florida. I own a second home there. It used to be one of my favorite vacation spots with Justice."

Dre was surprised. "I never knew that."

"It's probably a lot of things about me you don't know," Felicia replied with a bitter chuckle.

Chapter Twenty Three

Asia and a stream of other female inmates lined up to use the phones. She waited patiently listening to a girl standing in front of her having phone sex. She prayed that the number she'd been reciting over and over in her head for the past few minutes was the right one for Divine. She'd spent one night in jail and desperately needed to reach him before her arraignment in a few hours.

As soon as the judge grants me bail, I need him to be here with some cash so I can take off these hideous orange scrubs and walk outta this fucking place, she thought to herself.

When it was finally her turn, Asia stepped up to reach for the phone, but a tall, manly looking woman with a short buzz cut, and big lips blocked her path.

"It's my turn to use it," she snarled.

Knowing this was her only time to call Divine, Asia wasn't about to back down, especially since this was her first time being able to call someone due to overcrowding the night before. "You better back your big burly ass the fuck up. Don't let the pretty face fool you, bitch!" Asia responded back.

The woman stood there for a second looking Asia up and down. She then smiled. "Oohhh, talking shit turns me on. I likes the fact that you didn't back down like all these other weak ass women," she said, blowing Asia a kiss and backing away.

Asia eyeballed her as she grabbed the phone receiver off the wall making sure the woman wasn't up to anything. The woman smiled again, this time it was so wide you could see several gold teeth in the front of her mouth.

"And you's a smart cautious bitch, too. I likes that. Until we meet again sexy," the woman said, pimping away like a dude.

Asia shook her head thinking, *I gotta get the fuck out of here A.S.A.P.*

She quickly dialed Divine's number. When she heard the female recorder say, *please enjoy the ringtone while waiting for your party to answer* followed by his new single *Get Money* blasting in the phone, Asia knew she had the right number. It was her first glimpse of hope.

"Hello," Divine answered on the third ring.

"You have a collect call from the Dade County Jail. To accept this call, press five," the automated operator spoke.

Asia waited patiently, hoping Divine would accept the call. As soon as she heard him say hello once again, she let out a small sigh of relief.

"Hey, Divine, thank God you picked up your phone. Listen, I'm in trouble and really need your help. As you can see, I'm locked up and I was wondering if you could please come bail me out? I don't know what my bail is gonna be yet since I'm about to go to this arraignment, but it shouldn't be that much. I can pay you back once I get out. I'm about to come into a lot of money," she pleaded.

Divine was quiet for a minute. "Asia, I'm not bailing your sorry ass out of jail. The only reason why I even answered was because I thought the call was from my cousin. I heard all about what you did to my boy, Zoe. Me and that nigga go way back. We like brothers, actually. I can't believe you robbed him then had the nerve to invite the nigga to your hotel room after you turned me down."

"What? I didn't invite him to my room. He followed me to my room. He raped me Divine!" Asia screamed into the phone.

Divine laughed, "Yeah right. Y'all money hungry bitches are all the same. When you can't get any money from a nigga, first thing you do is holla rape. Get the fuck outta here, you bum bitch!" he said, laughing as he hung up the phone in her face.

Asia held the receiver in her hand. She was shocked at the way Divine had talked to her. Even worse, she knew Divine was the only person she had to call to help her out. There was no one else. She also wished she had enough money to hire Toni Vaughn, or another top notch attorney to represent her. Possibly facing child abandonment and endangerment charges, Asia knew she was gonna need a good attorney to help her get out and regain custody of her son.

"Are you finished? Other people need to use the phone," a female inmate yelled out.

Instead of getting into any type of altercation, Asia hung up the phone and stepped away with her head hung low as she proceeded back to her three-walled concrete cell.

I got to get out of here so I can go get my son. I was so close to getting my money and being set for life. Her chain of thought was suddenly broken when she bumped into the Amazon woman again. *I'm definitely not in the mood to keep dealing with this dike bitch.*

"Pretty girl, I don't think we've been properly introduced. My name is Moe and I runs this place. Anything I wants I gets in here," she said, rubbing Asia on her face.

Quickly moving her head back, Asia displayed a look of disapproval. She almost threw up in her mouth from the strong, rancid scent coming from the woman's body, and Asia wanted to tell her so badly that she didn't need to keep adding an extra "s" to most of her words.

"Let me know if you needs anything in here. I'm known to make shit happen," the woman stated just before tapping Asia on the ass.

At that moment Asia became furious. In her mind it was the ultimate sign of disrespect for someone who wasn't gay. It was about to go down as Asia clenched her fist and prepared herself mentally and physically for a fight. But just as she attempted to confront the woman, a C.O. walked up.

"Inmate 941207Asia Jones, let's go, it's time for your arraignment."

Saved by the bell, Asia thought as she watched the C.O. cuff her hands, then followed him down the hall to the elevator. While waiting, she admired how cute he was and noticed that he wasn't wearing a wedding ring.

"Why isn't a handsome man like yourself married?" she asked.

He looked back at Asia. "Who said I wasn't married?"

"I don't see a wedding band on your finger," Asia flirted. Even though she was locked up some things would never change.

"I am married. I just don't wear my ring to work," he responded as the elevator doors opened and they walked inside.

"Well, she's a lucky woman. I wish I had run into you on the outside. You would've been asking her for a divorce," Asia joked.

"Is that right?"

"That's right. I got what's called platinum pussy baby."

This time the C.O. didn't respond. The expression on his face made it obvious that he believed the conversation was getting out of hand. Once they finally reached the lower level and the elevator doors opened, he escorted Asia out of a back door and into a van where several other inmates were also waiting to go to court. She sat in the van looking at the other women wondering what crime they'd committed. Asia didn't consider herself a criminal and couldn't believe she had to be in such close quarters with possible murderers.

During the short ride to the court building, her mind was fixated on a plan to get out. But with no money, it was beginning to look like a difficult task. Even the money she'd stolen from the white guy might not have been enough. Not to mention, the police hadn't allowed Asia to retrieve her purse from the hotel room the night she was arrested, so she was sure it had been stolen by now.

When the van pulled up at the courthouse a few minutes later, Asia along with the other female inmates were escorted inside on a back elevator and up to a waiting room until it was time for them to see the judge. Several agonizing minutes later, Asia was the first to be called. Her stomach did all sorts of somersaults as a court officer escorted her into the courtroom and sat her down at a table.

Asia lowered her head in disbelief. The entire time she'd been in Miami, Asia was determined to get inside a courtroom, but not this way. She was supposed to be on the plaintiff side with a huge smile on her face once the judge told her the amount she'd be getting from Sandino. Now, Asia was the defendant, facing possible jail time for something that she knew she was guilty of.

"I just need my bond to be as low as possible, so I can have a chance at getting out," Asia said with her head still lowered. She was too embarrassed to look up.

Suddenly the baliff blurted out, "All rise, this court is now in session. The Honorable Judge Randolph is presiding."

Asia stood up, still focusing on the old wooden table as the judge entered the court room and took a seat at his bench.

"You may be seated," the judge responded.

Another court officer then called out a docket number and yelled, "People versus Asia Jones!"

The officer escorted Asia up in front of the judge as he took a minute to review her file. When he finally looked up, his facial expression immediately changed. His face seemed completely flushed.

"So, we meet again, Ms. Jones."

Asia looked like she'd seen a ghost when she realized the judge was the man she'd robbed two days prior. She suddenly felt sick to her stomach and weak at the knees when beads of sweat quickly formed on her forehead.

Oh my God. I'm fucked, she thought.

The judge smirked before continuing. "Ms. Jones, you have been charged with one count of child abandonment, one count of child endangerment and one count of child neglect. How do you plead?"

Asia wanted to say something, but couldn't get the words out.

"How do you plead, Ms. Jones." he asked again.

She cleared her throat. "Umm…not guilty, Your Honor. I didn't do anything wrong. I really need to get out so I can go get my son."

"Is this the same son that you left alone in a hotel?" the judge asked.

Asia looked at him with a dumbfounded look on her face. "It didn't happen the way those people in the hotel are saying it did."

Several of the people in the courtroom looked at her with disgust. Regardless of what her reason or excuse was, when cases involved children, bystanders were usually non-forgiving. The judge obviously wasn't buying it either.

Moments later, the clerk interrupted by passing the judge a piece of paper. After reading it, he blurted out, "Bail denied, Ms. Jones. You will be held in Dade County until your next court date."

Asia freaked out. "Are you serious? Why? I need to get out of here."

"And so does every other inmate who appears before me," the judge shot back. "Do you have a criminal defense attorney?"

"No," Asia mumbled.

"Well, a public defender will be assigned to your case." At that moment, the judge saw one of the worst lawyers in the state of Florida walk into the courtroom. Once again, a smirk appeared on his face.

He never wins any of his cases. After what that bitch did to me he would be perfect to represent her, he thought to himself.

"Mr. Currie, are you representing anyone today?" the judge questioned before placing the piece of paper inside her folder.

The lawyer looked around surprised by the question. "Yes, but my next case isn't until noon, Your Honor."

"In that case, I'll need you to represent Ms. Jones. We can deal with all the proper procedure paperwork later." He pointed to Asia. "Please discuss these charges with her," he said, holding up Asia's file.

"Okay, Your Honor," the lawyer replied with a puzzled look, but didn't ask any questions.

The judge looked down at Asia. "Normally you get your court appointed attorney before your next court date, but I've decided to bend the rules a little and appoint one to you now. Besides, it looks like you're really going to need it."

Asia was shocked as the officer escorted her out of the courtroom and into a small back room. After sitting down, the lawyer introduced himself.

"Hello Ms. Jones, my name is Chris Currie and it looks like I've been assigned as your court appointed attorney."

Asia shook his hand with her cuffs on. She looked the man up and down. Wearing a cheap, pin stripe suit, and black wire frame glasses, it looked like he was fresh out of law school. Still wet behind the ears.

I hope he knows what he's doing. But then again who am I to be picky. It's not like I can afford anybody else anyway, she thought.

"Okay, Ms. Jones, so…" the lawyer attempted to say.

"Wait, I have a question. Do you know if the judge has a wife?" Asia asked as she suddenly thought about her black-mail scheme. Even though her phone was also left inside the hotel, Asia thought it might've been someway her cell provider could retrieve the pictures. It was a long shot, but worth looking into.

"I'm not sure how that information is beneficial to your case Ms Jones."

"It's not, but since you're my lawyer now I need you to do what I say," Asia demanded.

The young attorney seemed intimidated. He stared at Asia before pushing up his glasses. "Judge Randolph's wife died two years ago."

Asia lowered her head once again. Every plan she had, seemed to fail.

"How the hell could he not give me a bail? Isn't it something you can do? Are you going to be able to get me off on those charges?" she asked.

Chris looked through the file handed to him from the judge then grabbed a pen from his briefcase. "Well, Ms. Jones, it seems like you have a much bigger problem now."

Asia sat up straight in the chair. "What are you talking about?"

"As you know when you were arrested and processed they took your fingerprints."

"Yeah."

"Well, it looks as if your fingerprints came back as a match to an ongoing murder investigation."

Asia frowned. "Murder Investigation? What the hell are you talking about? No, Mr. Currie, I'm afraid you may have it all wrong. You heard the judge. I'm here for child abandon-ment, endangerment and neglect."

"Yes, originally you were, but now it looks as if you

might be facing a first or second degree murder charge."

"Whoa, whoa, what the fuck did you just say?"

The lawyer paused, scratching his head. "Ms. Jones, it looks like your fingerprints were found at the scene of a murder for a ..." He fumbled through the papers in front of him. "Yes, sorry about that... here we are, for a Keon Moore. He was found dead in his home almost a year ago."

Asia closed her eyes as visions of the night she killed Keon flashed in her mind. She then rubbed her temples in a circular motion. Stress crept up on her within seconds.

"Are you okay, Ms. Jones? Did you know this man?" Chris questioned.

"Yes, I did. We dated for a short time, but I'm just taken back by the news that he's dead. We were really good friends. We would probably still be dating if I hadn't moved away. I spent a lot of time at his place so of course my finger prints would be there," Asia tried to convince.

The lawyer jotted down some notes, "I see... so it sounds like you... I mean we are gonna have to prove this."

"If I just told you that I used to date him and spent time over there can't you tell them that my fingerprints will probably be all over that crime scene? Aren't you supposed to be my lawyer? Do some damn work and get me off on these bullshit charges," she said, grabbing him by the shirt. An officer pulled her away within seconds.

The lawyer's face turned beet red as he quickly began stuffing papers back into his briefcase. He then rose from the table and walked out of the room without saying another word.

Asia immediately broke down crying, *Oh God, what if they give me the death penalty? I didn't mean to do all the bad things I've done in my life. I regret mistreating my son, killing Keon, and stealing money from so many people. I just ask for forgiveness because it looks like my life is over and I'm about to rot in this place.*

LIFE *After* A BALLA

Chapter Twenty Four

Felicia, who had just taken over as the driver, yawned and she pulled into the driveway of her three bedroom home on Harbor Island. It normally took anybody doing the speed limit almost ten hours, but Dre who drove over eighty-miles per hour the entire time got them there in nine, including the two times they'd stopped for restroom and food breaks. She pressed the garage remote and pulled into the two car garage, before parking the car and turning off the ignition. Instantly all the memories of the many summer vacations she and Justice spent there flashed into her mind. When Felicia felt the water building up in her eyes, she closed them tight trying to fight back tears.

How did things end up like this Justice? I did every-thing right in our relationship and you still left me. If you would've loved me the way I loved you, we would still be to-gether right now.

Felicia was so deep in thought she didn't hear Dre call-ing her name.

"Felicia…Felicia, shake that shit off, we got business to handle. Now ain't the time to get all sentimental on me!" he warned.

She delivered several sighs, and then rolled her eyes in

Jackie D.

a manner that should have informed Dre that she didn't appreciate being talked to that way. Dre was on a mission and had already removed Kareem from the front seat and waited for her to open the door. Even though Dre had decided not to keep him in the trunk very long, Kareem's hands were still tied and his mouth was still covered with tape.

"Hurry the fuck up, Felicia!" he barked.

Felicia eyebrows rose and her expression went soar. "I don't know who you think you're yelling at, Dre. I'm not a child. I've had enough of your mouth for one fucking day. Don't rush me!" she shot back.

She leaned down and put her feet back inside her heels, then got out of the car. When Felicia walked past Dre, she slung her huge designer purse over her shoulder hitting him as she put the key inside the door. Just like her house back in Georgia, Felicia's vacation home was just as beautiful. The one story home had soaring twenty-five foot ceilings, expensive hardwood flooring and a gorgeous gourmet kitchen. Not to mention the top of the line furniture she'd decorated with.

"Do you have to use the bathroom?" Dre asked Kareem. When Kareem shook his head back and forth, Dre responded with, "good." He grabbed one of the chairs out of the dining room, told Kareem to sit down, then tied his legs to the chair, "Now, I'm gonna remove this tape, but if you make any noise that I don't approve of, the shit is goin' back on." When he snatched the tape off, Kareem winced from the pain, but didn't make a sound.

Dre didn't waste anytime removing the gun from his waist. "Now, time to make that call," he said, pointing the firearm at Kareem's forehead with one hand and handing him his cell phone with the other.

Kareem let out a huge sigh before dialing the number.

Felicia, who was still pissed off, walked into the bedroom and closed the door so she could change her clothes. After getting comfortable in a pair of shorts and a tank top, she

Jackie D.

sat on the bed. She was having second thoughts about the whole thing, especially now since Dre's intentions didn't seem good.

"Felicia, come in here. I gotta go meet the nigga, Cruze. I need you to watch him until I get back!" Dre yelled. When she didn't respond he walked right into the bedroom without even knocking. "Did you hear me?"

Felicia just nodded her head. She was tired and wanted to go to sleep to make this whole nightmare go away.

"Look mannn…I apologize for the way I've been talkin' to you Felicia, but this shit got me stressed out. I need you right now. We almost got what we've been waitin' for. Please don't quit on me now. Can you go in the livin' room and watch him," he pleaded.

Without saying a word, she got up off the bed and walked back into the living room.

Dre followed then leaned over Kareem, whispering in his ear. "Remember nigga, your family is on the line, so don't fuck up." He then looked at Felicia. "Don't worry, I'll be back soon," he said just before grabbing the keys and walking out the door.

Felicia was starving but knew it was nothing in the house to eat since she hadn't been there in almost a year. She didn't really care about the house being fully stocked with food, but she did care about its cleanliness. Felicia had house-keepers come twice a month to make sure the place was kept up to her standards.

She leaned against the oversized island in the kitchen and crossed her arms trying to decide on what to do about food. When she glanced over at the refrigerator and saw a number for pizza delivery, she grabbed the phone and ordered two large pizza's and a two liter Sprite. When she looked over at Kareem who was staring her down but not saying a word, she pulled her eyes away from him and walked back inside her room to wait for the food. It was hard enough that she was

Jackie D.

having second thoughts about the situation, and his saddened puppy dog look wasn't making matters any better.

"Just remember what Dre said about you making any noise when that pizza guy gets here. Don't try anything," she still decided to say.

Thirty minutes later, Felicia emerged from the foyer of the house with two white boxes in her hand. She placed the boxes on the table, grabbed some ice and two cups to pour the soda in from out the kitchen and sat down. Opening the box, Felicia grabbed a slice then reached over and placed it in Kareem's mouth.

"Thank you Le Le...I mean Felicia," he said while chewing. "So...you're a doctor, huh?"

Felicia showed a slight grin. "Yeah."

"I just thought about the lab coat I saw in your closet. That also explains your bank account balance. The day you left me that note, you must've accidently wrote it on the back of your bank statement. I was so excited to have me a paid girl-friend."

Once again, Felicia grinned.

"Look, can I ask you something? Did you ever have any true feelings for me?"

She looked over at him, feeling bad for misleading someone who obviously cared for her at one point. "I never meant to hurt you, Kareem. I just wanted to know what hap-pened to my husband," Felicia said, giving him another bite of pizza.

"You didn't answer my question," Kareem replied still staring at her.

"Kareem, you're a really sweet guy, but the only man I have ever loved since I was in high school has been Justice. I just have so many unanswered questions regarding his disap-pearance and possible death." Felicia lowered her head.

Kareem chewed the food that was in his mouth before speaking again."It's cool. I apologize for putting my hands on

Jackie D.

you. I promised myself I would never hit a woman after seeing my father abuse my mother for years and I ended up acting just like him. And with that said, I'll tell you whatever you wanna know Felicia."

She anxiously sat up and put the food down thinking, *finally!*

"Do you think Justice really loved your mother?" she questioned.

Kareem shrugged his shoulders. "I don't know, he told her he did all the time. He pursued her really hard and my mother didn't know anything about you at first. When she did find out that Justice was married she ended the relationship immediately. And he wasn't happy about it at all. He kept calling, but she wouldn't take him back. He told her he didn't love you, he loved her."

Felicia felt like she'd been stabbed in the heart after hearing that Justice really loved Skye.

"Then somehow Justice teamed up with my dad, for money obviously and led him straight to where we lived. We'd been hiding from him for months. That dreadful night is forever etched in my mind," Kareem said, closing his eyes and shaking his head.

"What happened? Is that the night Justice was killed?"

"Yes, I remember listening as my mother and Justice argued. She told him to leave and he got up and opened the door. Minutes later my dad walked in and immediately told my mom that Justice had sold us out for money. He was getting ready to try and beat her again, and that's when I ran out of the room pointing a gun at him. I yelled for him to leave, but of course he didn't."

Felicia sat listening in shock. The more she listened, the more upset she became. She could tell Kareem was getting emotional as he continued with the story.

"My dad jumped and tried to grab the gun from me causing it to go off. A few seconds later Justice fell to the floor.

Jackie D.

He got hit by a stray bullet in his chest," Kareem admitted. "So, you see, your husband's death was an accident, in fact it was his own fault for being greedy. My dad used to say all the time that money will make you do crazy shit! I guess he was right about something for once. Felicia, my mother was just the victim. I swear I don't know what Cruze did with the body. After that night we all vowed to never talk about it again."

Felicia sat speechless. She'd finally gotten the truth about what really happened to Justice and it wasn't at all what she expected. She wondered if Justice ever really loved her or if their entire marriage was all a lie and he'd just stayed for the financial benefits.

A single tear raced down her face and traveled into her mouth. She pressed her lips together to catch it. She had her answer and as much as it hurt, Felicia was glad to have closure. Now, it didn't matter to her either way if they ever found the body.

Maybe you got what you deserved, Mr. Justice Mitchell, she thought.

Dre pulled up at the small bar that Cruze told Kareem to meet him at. It took some time but he had finally remembered where he knew the name Cruze from. Sandino had showed him a picture and frequently talked about Cruze when they were locked up together. He used to say how they'd been friends since childhood and that he trusted him with his life.

"I bet Sandino feels stupid now. He probably never expected his good friend to steal his wife and family."

Dre parked the car and went inside. Noticing how small and secluded the place was, he scanned the room and spotted Cruze sitting at a table in the corner.

"You Cruze, right?" Dre asked when he walked up.

Cruze looked Dre up and down. "Who wants to know?"

Jackie D.

"Kareem wants to know, nigga," Dre shot back.

"What the fuck is this shit about? Where's Kareem?" Cruze yelled.

Dre looked around to see if the few people in the bar had heard the loud outburst. When he realized that they couldn't hear over the music playing he responded. "He's alive and in a safe place and he'll stay that way as long as you cooperate. My brother was Justice, and I already know that you killed him. But what I don't know is what the fuck you did wit' his body. I need you to take me to him."

Cruze glanced around the bar making sure no one heard him being accused of murder. "I don't know what the fuck you talking about. I didn't kill Justice and I'm not taking you anywhere.'

Dre leaned over in his face and pulled his shirt exposing his gun. "Well, if you don't take me you can tell that bitch Skye to kiss her son goodbye!"

Jackie D.

Chapter Twenty Five

Skye paced the floor of her bedroom worried sick because she hadn't been able to get in touch with Kareem. After driving home from the lunch date with Cruze, she began calling to see if he wanted to talk, but still hadn't gotten an answer. Despite whatever problems they had, Kareem never ignored Skye's calls and always called her back if he was busy, so this only increased her concern. She'd even left a message for Cruze telling him to call her back, but hadn't heard from him either. Skye's motherly instinct told her that something was wrong.

"I think I'm gonna have to break down and call Cruze again," Skye said. "I pray he's not salty about me walking out on him at the restaurant. If so, he needs to get over that shit, because this is important."

She picked her phone up off the bed and dialed his number, but his time instead of ringing it went straight to voicemail. This made Skye even more anxious.

"Cruze, I'm worried about Kareem. I haven't been able to get in touch with him since he called me, and I'm worried. I know he was supposed to call you and I'm wondering if you ever heard from him. Please call me back as soon as you get this," she said, ending the call.

As Skye continued to pace the floor, part of her felt guilty for leaving her son in Georgia by himself. *What was I suppose to do? If he didn't want to come I couldn't make him,* she thought.

Feeling like a panic attack was approaching, Skye grabbed her purse and took out her Ativan. She hadn't taken the pills in months, but with thoughts of not being able to get to her son who was six hundred miles away entered her mind, it felt like she needed to take the entire bottle in order to calm down.

Skye left her room and headed downstairs to get a glass of water. When she walked into the kitchen, she saw a note from Quinn taped to the refrigerator stating that he'd run out to pick up a few supplies for Sandino. Not really caring, Skye shrugged her shoulders, grabbed a bottle of Deer Park and popped two pills.

With the house so quiet she could hear Jordan having a conversation with Sandino in his room. Hearing the excitement in his voice, it hurt Skye's feelings knowing he was trying to form a new relationship, especially since Jordan hadn't been talking to her much since their little argument. Jordan had even started to help Quinn by taking on a lot of the responsibilities with Sandino. She'd even noticed him going into Sandino's room almost every day.

As soon as Skye heard Jordan laughing, she decided to go eavesdrop at the door to hear what they were talking about. She stood listening to Jordan talk about his football team in Georgia and his new team in Miami and how he liked his new team better. She then peeked inside and could see Payton sitting on Jordan's lap smiling at Sandino, who was enjoying every minute of the bonding. When Jordan passed him some of the pictures she'd taken at one of his championship games in Georgia, Sandino started grunting, trying to point to something on the picture. Jordan looked over at the picture to see what he was talking about.

"Dad, Kareem stayed in Georgia with his girlfriend. Hopefully he will come to visit soon. I never thought I would miss him but I do," Jordan said.

Skye walked away thinking, *I miss him too Jordan, and I hope he's alright.*

About an hour later, Skye was laying across her bed watching an episode of Law and Order on T.V. The medication had relaxed her a bit.

"Maybe Kareem made up with Le Le and they took a trip somewhere. She'd been trying to get him to go out of town and since I'm not around her old ass is probably working her magic on my poor innocent son. I hope he doesn't come back married or saying that I'm gonna be a grandmother. My heart can't take that shit right now," Skye said out loud.

Her thoughts were suddenly shifted when she felt her phone vibrate against the nightstand. Thinking it might be Kareem, Skye got really excited. Jumping up, she quickly retrieved the phone and looked at the caller ID. When she saw that it was Toni Vaughn, her excitement instantly turned to disappointment.

"Oh my God, what is it now? Seems like every time she calls its bad news," Skye said in frustration. She answered it anyway. "Hello."

"Hello Skye, how are you?"

"I could be better."

"Oh, I'm sorry to hear that."

"So, what's up, Toni?" Skye responded in a rushed tone.

"Well, I hope you're sitting down. The DNA results came back and it looks as if the chances of Sandino being the father of Asia Jones' baby is 99%."

Skye shook her head. "Wow."

"Now, I know you and Ms. Jones aren't on the best of terms right now, but since you were once friends I hope you all can get along for the sake of the child."

Skye took a deep breath. Just the mere mention of Asia's name irritated her. She wanted to go off on Toni and tell her that she didn't give a damn about Asia or the baby, but decided to hold her composure. Instead of responding, she just shook her head in disbelief and continued to listen.

"Also, I have more news. I just found out that Asia is locked up for child abandonment. Apparently she left her son alone in her hotel room. The baby is currently in the custody of Child Protective Services."

Skye laughed out loud. "You've got to be kidding me. I knew that bitch couldn't take care of a baby."

"I'm not sure what Ms. Jones' situation is in regards to her release, but since Sandino is the biological father he has the legal right to try and obtain custody of the child, especially now since he can prove that she's an unfit mother. You and I both know that Sandino loves his kids more than anything and I don't think he would treat this child any differently. He bragged to me all the time about how much of a good mother you were. I just think you need to put your personal feelings for Asia aside and think about the best interest of this child. Remember…you're a mother also. I'm sure if something ever happened to you, God forbid, you would want your kids to be cared for by great parents in a good home. Besides this would be such good press for Sandino."

Skye started stuttering. "So…what the fuck are you trying to say, Toni? Are you implying that I take care of Asia's baby? Oh hell no…nope…not me... and Sandino damn sure can't!"

"Skye, please calm down."

"Hell no. I can't believe you called me with that bullshit. Who gives a fuck about how good Sandino would look in the press. I don't care about that! Besides, you telling me to get along with Asia is personal advice, not legal!"

"Skye, it's obvious that I've upset you, so I'll give you some time to think it over. I'll call you later in the week."

"Don't even bother," Skye said, hanging up in Toni's face.

Rage took over Skye's body all over again as all the bad things that happened to her at the hands of Sandino appeared in her mind. She turned around and ran back downstairs. When Skye hit the last few steps she tripped and tumbled down onto the floor. This pissed her off even more. Picking herself up, she stormed into Sandino's room past Jordan and Payton. All she wanted to do was beat Sandino's ass. It was almost as if Skye had an out of body experience as she started hitting Sandino in his face with several hard blows.

"Its official, you now have a third son, Sandino Jr.! For some crazy reason I thought it was a possibility that Asia could be making this shit up to try and get money. But I should've known two snakes would end up in the same fucking hole. I hate you, Sandino! It's because of you that this family is broken! It's because of you that Kareem didn't want to come home. It's because of you that he could possibly be missing!" she screamed with high-pitched intensity.

Jordan jumped up with Payton hanging onto him for dear life as Skye kept hitting Sandino with tears flowing down her face.

"Ma, stop it! All that stuff is in the past. I don't know who you are anymore. How do you function carrying all that stuff around? All that hate... all that anger?"

Skye stopped and backed away crying uncontrollably. "You just don't understand, Jordan. You haven't been through what I have been through!"

"Ma, I been right there with you. I've seen it all. If I can forgive him, can't you? We should've never come back here if you can't forgive and move on. And what do you mean Kareem is missing?" Jordan questioned.

All of a sudden, Skye and Jordan saw Sandino struggling trying to say something. When he was finally able to get the words out he looked at Skye and said, "Sorryyyy, I love youuuu."

He let out several loud grunts then started shaking and having convulsions as his eyes rolled back into his head. They could tell he was having another seizure.

"I told Quinn not to leave this house for a long time and the minute he does, look what the fuck happens," Skye said to herself .

"Ma, look what you did. Are you trying to kill him?" Jordan yelled passing Payton to Skye and running to his father's aide.

Sandino's body started to slide down in his chair, making it easier for Jordan to get him to the floor. He pulled one of the plush decorative pillows from the bed and placed it under his head and shifted him onto his side. He'd watched Quinn do this numerous times to keep Sandino from choking.

"Do something, Ma!" Jordan held his father's head as it shook uncontrollably and he foamed from the mouth.

Suddenly, the seizure stopped as quickly as it started. Skye just stood motionless watching. Moments later, Jordan panicked when he realized his father stopped breathing.

Chapter Twenty Six

Dre and Cruze rode in complete silence back to Felicia's vacation house. Curiosity was killing Dre as he wondered how Cruze could double cross Sandino, who considered him his best friend, by stealing his wife. He decided to ask him about it mainly because he was tired of the silence and he was also getting sleepy. He hadn't been to sleep in almost twenty-four hours.

"Cruze, I've heard a lot about you, how you used to be the man in the streets back in the day."

Cruze looked at Dre wondering how he knew things about his past and why he was even trying to make conversation with him in the first place.

"Yeah man, Sandino and I were cell mates when he was locked up and he talked about you all time. He expected you to come visit him, but you never did. He considers you family," Dre went on to say.

Cruze didn't respond, but looked out the window instead.

"He really trusted you and probably never expected you to steal his damn wife. That's some fucked up shit to do to the man knowin' he's down and out." Dre shook his head like he was thinking about something. "But shitttt now that I think about it, Skye is fine as a muthafucka. When I saw her for the first time I almost lost my mind. She shoulda been in a beauty pageant or some shit like that. Plus, the bitch got a fat ass, too! Umm, umm, umm, I see why Sandino kept her on lock down for all those years."

Cruze could feel his temperature rising as Dre talked about Skye.

If only I knew where Kareem was, I would pull my fucking gun out right now and blow his ass away, Cruze thought.

He just bit down on his lip and continued to ignore him thinking about how much he loved Skye and once he got Kareem home safely he wasn't leaving her side no matter what she said this time. He'd seen it in her eyes at the restaurant. He could tell how much she really wanted to take him back, but was still hurt and her pride wouldn't allow it. He planned to prove to her that he was willing to do whatever it took to show her just how much he loved her… even if it meant killing for her again.

When they arrived at Felicia's house several minutes later, Cruze suddenly had that sinking feeling in the pit of his stomach that he got every time something bad was about to happen. He wished he could call Skye but Dre had insisted that he turn off his phone before even agreeing to take him to Kareem.

I just hope we can get out of here alive, hopefully that won't be a problem since I'm packing. I can't believe the stupid muthafucka didn't even bother to check me for a weapon, he thought.

Dre hit the button on the remote to activate the garage door. "Let me remind you not to try nothin' stupid when we get in here. As soon as you see that nigga, I wanna know where my brother is."

Agreeing to his demands, Cruze followed Dre' inside the house. He could hear the T.V. playing in the livingroom area and wondered whose place it was since it looked like the owner had money. Felicia had fallen asleep on the couch after talking to Kareem but quickly woke up when she heard the garage door opening. She hoped Dre had gotten the information he needed from Cruze so they could let Kareem go and leave. She was ready for the whole thing to be over with.

Kareem immediately became nervous. "Felicia listen…if I don't make it out of here alive. Promise me you'll tell my mom I love her and that I'm sorry for giving her such a hard time," he whispered."

Felicia sat up and looked at Kareem in his eyes for the first time since he beat her. "You'll be able to tell her yourself. Dre's not going to hurt you. All he wants is the location of the body," she reassured him.

Seconds later, Dre walked into the living room and Felicia was surprised to see that he wasn't alone. Cruze scanned the room for Kareem and his eyes widened when he saw him tied up to a chair with bruises on his face.

"Kareem, you alright?" he asked.

"I'm good, Cruze. What are you doing here? You should've just told him what he wanted to know," Kareem said with concern.

Cruze was just about to walk over to Kareem, but Dre beat him to it and pointed his gun to Kareem's head.

Cruze paused trying to decide if he should reach for the gun inside in pants. "Let Kareem go, he didn't have anything to do with the murder," Cruze pleaded.

"Shut the fuck up! I'm tired of waiting, where's my brothers body?" Dre asked.

Cruze rubbed his head. He knew if they wanted to make it out of there he didn't have a choice but to tell him.

"Where is it?" Dre asked again.

"Inside an abandoned glass factory out in Newnan, Georgia. If you need to know where Newnan is, then Google the shit cuz that's all I'm saying. Now, untie him," Cruze demanded.

Jackie D.

Dre smiled like a kid in the candy store once he finally had the information he'd been waiting for. "Nigga, you think you can just smoke my damn brother and walk away?"

Felicia finally spoke up. "I found out the entire story, Dre. Justice's death was an accident. He got killed by a stray bullet when Kareem and his father were scuffling over the gun."

"You can believe that shit if you want to, I don't," Dre said just before he pulled the trigger.

Felicia went completely ballistic and started screaming as Kareem's body slumped down in the chair. He'd been shot in the side of the head.

"You muthafucka!" Cruze yelled reaching for his gun. He pulled it out and pointed it at Dre who in return lifted his gun and shot Cruze first.

Dre stood and watched as Cruze's body fell to the floor. He then ran up and shot Cruze again, this time in the chest, aiming straight for his heart. By now, Felicia was hysterical and screaming at the top of her lungs.

"Oh my God…oh my God. Why did you kill them, Dre? You got the information you needed! I'm not going to jail for you!"

He walked over to Felicia and grabbed her tight trying to calm her down. "Listen to me and calm down. We had to take them out. That nigga Cruze had a reputation in the streets, he would've come after me. Trust me, you're not going to jail. Once we get that money all this will be forgotten. Go get your things together and call a cab to take you to the airport and get out of here. I'll clean up this mess, get rid of the bodies and meet you back in Georgia. Don't do anything or speak to anybody until you hear from me. Do you understand?"

Felicia nodded her head before taking off running to the bathroom and throwing up in the toilet. All she could think about was the fact that she was responsible for two people losing their lives. *I should've never asked Dre to help me. He's out of control.*

After getting herself together she called a cab and grabbed her suit case.

"I better get out of here before this fool tries to kill me next!"

Jackie D.

Chapter Twenty Seven

Skye stared watching the news as they talked about Sandino's death. She listened as they said, "Funeral arrangements have yet to be announced."

"Until I find Kareem, I'm not even thinking about burying Sandino," she said to herself.

As if it wasn't bad enough that the press was constantly staked out outside, Skye felt like she couldn't even turn on the T.V. without hearing Sandino's name. *If it were up to me, he would've been dead a long time ago.*

Her mind drifted back to Sandino's first night home. She remembered sneaking into his room and standing over him with a pillow ready to smother him as he slept. All her years of domestic, sexual and verbal abuse, danced in her head. When she heard Quinn moving around in his room across the hall, Skye finally snapped out of her trance. It was at that moment when she realized it would be too hard to explain Sandino's sudden death and going to jail was definitely out of the question. So, she quickly left the room.

Skye shook her head focusing her mind back on Kareem. *Why hasn't Cruze called me back about Kareem? I told him being back in the streets would interfere with him being there for his family and this is a prime example. Even If I did consider taking his ass back he can forget it now. He made his choice...the streets. Why did I think he was any different from all the other no good men I've had in my life?*

"Maybe I'm cursed!" she yelled.

Skye threw the remote across the room and quickly hopped up and caught a glimpse of her image in the mirror. Her eyes were bloodshot red and the puffy bags under lids now seemed to be permanent. She hadn't bathed or combed her hair in days and looked a complete mess. But for now appearances didn't matter. All she wanted to do was talk to Kareem. Four days had passed, and she still hadn't heard one word from him. She'd even called the Georgia Police Department and filed a missing person's report, but since Skye didn't even know Felicia's address, the police told her it was going to be even more difficult to find him. Now, she didn't know what else to do.

"I can't believe I was so consumed with getting back to Miami that I didn't even take the time to find out where Le Le lived or got her number."

Suddenly Skye heard a knock at her bedroom door.

"Who is it?" she yelled.

"Jordan!"

Skye was surprised. Jordan hadn't said a complete sentence to her since Sandino's fatal seizure.

It's not my fault he had the damn seizure. If he had left us alone and not come to my apartment that night we all would be just fine right now, she thought to herself. *As a father he was suppose to give his sons good life lessons, and good memories. Yet Sandino has left his sons with nothing but taunted memories. Sorry muthafucka.*

Not only that, Quinn was so upset that he wasn't around to possibly save Sandino, he packed up and left right after the Coroner's took away the body without even saying goodbye.

"I didn't like his punk ass any damn way," Skye mumbled before telling Jordan to come in.

Jordan walked in the room carrying Payton and sat on

the side of her bed. He looked really upset like he'd been crying.

"What's wrong? Are you alright?" Skye asked, grabbing Payton.

Jordan didn't say anything. Instead he stared Skye down with uncertainty. Seconds later, he broke down crying again. Skye put Payton down on the bed and reached over and grabbed her son.

"I know you're upset son and I'm sorry. I know you loved your father and were finally developing a relationship with him again. I told you it wasn't going to be easy coming back here. I've been thinking lately and I know now that I made the wrong choice. I was so worried about us struggling and being broke thinking if we came back for the money we would be happier. But in all honesty it seemed like we were happier without the money," Skye admitted.

Jordan lifted his head. "You're right. We were happier without all the money. We would still be together as a family. Me, you, Payton, Kareem and Cruze. You used to tell us that it wasn't healthy to carry around a grudge but you are. If leaving this house will make you turn back into my mom again then can we please leave tonight?"

At that moment Skye felt even worse. Realizing her son was right, she knew it was time to make some drastic changes.

Later that night, Skye heard the door bell ring. Thinking it was a reporter trying to get her statement about Sandino, she first decided to ignore it. But after looking out the window and realizing that all the paparazzi were camped out at the end of the driveway, Skye became excited hoping it might be Kareem. Running down the stairs, Skye kept visualizing how big her hug was going to be as soon as she saw his face. Skye knew at that point she never wanted to be without her kids, and would cherish them every day after this scare. Opening the door, her heart was filled with anticipation, until she looked at the person standing on the opposite side. She was surprised to see who it was.

"What are you doing here? How did you find out where I lived?" Skye asked.

Suddenly all the paparazzi ran up to the door, taking pictures.

"We need to talk," Felicia said. "Can I come in?"

Realizing the pictures of her would be all over the news, Skye quickly stepped to the side, allowing Felicia to enter. However, as soon as she closed the door, Skye immediately became alarmed because it looked as if Felicia had been crying for hours.

Skye's heart rate began to enhance. "Has something happened to my son, Le Le?"

Felicia looked up, then swallowed the huge lump in her throat. "My name isn't Le Le, Skye. It's Felicia...Felicia Mitchell. Justice was my husband."

Skye backed away. "What? Is this some type of joke? I need to talk to Kareem. Where is he? Where's my son?"

Tears formed in Felicia's eyes. She even opened her mouth, but nothing came out.

"Where is he? What happened to Kareem? Why are you here?" By this time tears were in Skye's eyes as well. "Answer me!"

"He's...he's dead," Felicia was barely able to say.

Skye immediately fell to her knees and wailed. "I knew it. I felt it."

Felicia ran over to Skye to comfort her.

"Get the fuck off me. It's all your fault! If it wasn't for you my son would be here in Miami with his family. I knew you were bad news the first day I laid eyes on you!" Anger and sadness consumed her body at the same time. If her son was dead, Felicia was gonna pay.

"I'm so sorry. I know you already hate me," Felicia said, sobbing uncontrollably.

Suddenly, Skye reached up and hit Felicia in the face then grabbed her hair, pulling her onto the floor. Within seconds, she'd gripped Felicia by her neck trying to cut off her air supply. Felicia fought back desperately trying to push Skye away. When she was finally able to loosen Skye's grip, the two rolled around on the floor fighting for what seemed like an eternity.

"You're right, it's all my fault. I should've helped him...I should've helped him," Felicia belted.

With no strength left to fight, Skye climbed off Felicia. They both laid side by side on the floor weeping.

"I'm so sorry," Felicia repeated.

"Who did this? Who kill him?"

"My husband's brother, Dre. He killed Kareem and Cruze."

Skye's heart dropped. "Oh my God Cruze is dead, too? No wonder he never called me back. Noooooo. What happened? Tell me what happened?"

"Cruze died trying to protect your son," Felicia informed. "Right before Kareem died he wanted me to tell you something. He wanted you to know how much he loved you and that he was sorry for everything."

Skye wailed again. "No...no...no. Please God, no."

"I just wanted to know what happened to Justice since the police didn't seem concerned. I told Dre I would give him half of Justice's life insurance money if he helped me so I could have closure. I'm so sorry Skye, I never meant for any of this to happen. I should've helped Kareem get away. But instead I watched Dre murder them both," she cried. "It took me days to finally get the courage to come over here and tell you. Dre would kill me if he knew I was here, but I don't care. I wanted you to know what happened. I didn't want you to go through the same thing I did."

Skye held a blank expression for what seemed forever. She was so happy that Jordan slept in such a comatose state because the last thing Skye wanted right now was for him to find out that his brother was gone. It felt like Skye's heart had been ripped out and shredded into tiny little pieces.

"So, you watched my son die?" Skye finally asked.

"Yeah, just like you watched my husband die," Felicia replied.

It was at the moment when Skye realized that they were both in the same position. She also realized that Felicia could've easily gone back to Georgia and never said a word. To Skye, the pain of not knowing what happened to her son would've been far too much to bear, so at the very moment she felt grateful.

"Seems like we both got something on each other, huh?" she said to Felicia. "Well, if you don't go to the police then neither will I."

Epilogue

One Year Later

Asia sat in the court room awaiting her verdict in a daze. It was almost as if she was having a bad dream or watching a *Lifetime* movie about somebody else's life instead of her own. In the past, she'd always managed to ease herself out of any tight situation that came her way. But karma had finally caught up with her. Out of all the bad things she'd done in her life she never expected to be in prison facing a second degree murder charge. Even though all the other charges had been dropped, and her attorney had requested that Judge Randolph not preside over the case, she knew that the new judge was planning to throw the book at her. He'd been eyeing her in a hateful way throughout the entire trial.

Guilt consumed Asia as she thought about her son. He was such a blessing from God and instead of slowing her lifestyle down and being a good mother, she'd allowed greed to get in the way, neglecting her beautiful baby boy. Her heart ached at the fact that she didn't know where he was or even have any pictures of him for memories.

I hope my son ends up with a good family that'll give him the love he deserved. I also hope that one day I'll get to see him again, she thought.

Minutes later, Asia stood as the verdict was about to be read. She closed her eyes and said quick prayer.

It's probably too late to ask for help God after all the wrong I've done, but please protect me right now, she thought.

The judge asked the jury if they reached a verdict.

"Yes sir, Your Honor," the jury foreman replied. When the bailiff passed a piece of paper to the judge, he looked at it then proceeded.

"On the count of murder in the second degree, we the jury find the defendant Asia Jones, guilty," he read.

You could hear the people's reaction throughout the courtroom.

"Asia Jones, you've been charged with second degree murder. Since your defense has requested an expedited sentencing I hereby sentence you to nineteen years, with eligibility for parole in eight. This sentence is to be served immediately at the Dade Correctional Institution," the judge stated.

As soon as he hit the gavel, Asia started crying uncontrollably. She always heard the saying, "If you do the crime you have to do the time," but she never thought it would apply to her. When the officers came over to handcuff her she collapsed onto the floor.

Felicia admired the panoramic view as she walked out the double French doors at her villa in Barbados. After giving Justice a proper burial and putting closure on that part of her life, she packed up and moved to the islands. It felt good to finally be moving on. After talking with Skye she was able to let go of the guilt she was carrying about Kareem's and Cruze's death as well.

She also disassociated herself from Dre and his negative energy. He'd used her during one of the worst times in her life and she planned to give him exactly what he deserved.

Dre arrived at Felicia's house all smiles. Although she'd been very distant towards him ever since the murders, today was the day the check was due to arrive from Justice's life insurance policy, so she'd called and told him to come by to get what he'd earned. Happy that Felicia had kept her word, Dre put the key inside the door and walked inside. The smile he'd been consuming all day instantly faded when he realized the house was empty. His mouth dropped. The only thing left was the fire place poker set. At that moment, it was obvious things weren't gonna go as planned.

In a fit of rage, Dre took his fist and hit the wall leaving a huge hole in the plaster. "If it wasn't for me she wouldn't have that fuckin' life insurance money!" he belted.

When he looked towards the kitchen and saw a white envelope on the counter he walked over and grabbed it. Suddenly, he became anxious and excited when he saw his name on the envelope. *Oh shit, I was gettin' upset for nothin'. Felicia must've left the check here*, he thought.

Dre opened the envelope with all smiles once again. However, instead of a check inside there was a small piece of paper that read:

Who would've ever thought you did this all for the money. I hope your ulterior motive was worth it. You get nothing, murderer!

Skye sat on the couch in her new home in Daytona Beach, Florida with a bottle of wine listening to music and crying. She looked up at the huge picture of Kareem hanging over her fire place. It was his birthday.

Jackie D.

She raised her hand, making a toast as the tears flowed heavily. "Here's to you my oldest son. I miss you so much."

Burying her first born son had proven to be one of the hardest things she'd ever done in her life. On the other hand, Skye was happy that Felicia was later able to convince Dre to tell her where Kareem's body was a week after his death. However, he refused to tell her where Cruze was.

Felicia anonymously called the police so they could locate Kareem, but as of today they still hadn't found Cruze. Because Cruze was the one responsible for hiding Justice's body, Skye could only assume this was the reason why Dre wouldn't reveal the whereabouts. Either way, Skye vowed to never give up looking for him because Cruze deserved a proper burial.

Kareem and Sandino were buried together side by side in a two person mausoleum at Visa Memorial Gardens. At first Skye went to visit every week, but as time passed she was able to let go and stopped going as often. The tears flowing down her face were not only sad tears but happy ones as well. After hearing Kareem's last words from Felicia, she knew her son loved her and died trying to protect his family just as he always promised to do.

With the help of a therapist, she was no longer taking medication and a much happier person. She'd even forgiven Sandino and Cruze in her heart and let go of all the hatred that once consumed her. She was rich, single, free and enjoying life without a man. Right now she was only interested in being the best mother she could be to her kids and looking forward to starting out fresh in a new city.

After taking another sip of her wine, she glanced over at a huge stack of mail forwarded from the old house that she'd picked up from the post office earlier that day. She flipped through the stack of mail which was mostly old bills until she came across a letter that was post marked from Jamaica. With widened eyes, Skye quickly tore open the envelope as an enormous grin formed on her face.

Hello me child. I have been trying to reach ya for somtime now. I hope you and me kids are ok and I hope de letter will reach ya in good health. When I heard about Mr. Sandino I decided to try and reach ya once again. I pray it works this time. Please call me.

Miss ya much.

Respect, Ms. Petra

Looking at Ms. Petra's phone number over and over like it couldn't be true, Skye grabbed her phone to call her travel agent. She and the kids were going on a much needed vacation to Jamaica. However, before she could dial, Skye listened as Jordan walked into the house along with the pitter patter of four additional little feet. After losing three people who were dear to her heart, Skye had a change of heart and went to Child Protective Services to get Sandino Jr. Since then she'd even applied for adoption so he would be raised as a Washington, the way Sandino would have wanted.

Jordan along with Payton and SJ walked into the living room a few minutes later and all snuggled beside her on the couch.

As SJ looked at her and said, "Ma Ma," his innocent little face warmed her heart. To him Skye was the only mother he knew. She told herself that maybe when he was older she'd take him to see Asia.

"Let's wish your brother a happy birthday," she said to everyone while pointing at Kareem's pictures. After counting to three, she and Jordan yelled, "Happy Birthday," while the little ones just smiled.

AN EXCERPT FROM *WEALTHY & WICKED* BY: CHRIS RENEE

Prologue

My eyes opened wide to the sight of the white ceiling. The bright lights caused a temporary fog as I tried to shake away the numbing pain that exploded in my brain.

"Well, it looks like my patient is awake," the voice said from the other side of the room. I tried to turn my head towards it but I had no strength left in my body.

"What do you mean patient? Where am I?" I couldn't remember much of anything before this moment. I tried my hardest to figure out how she had gotten me in this position.

"You're my patient. And in very good hands." She walked towards me with a long needle in her hand and a sinister smile on her face. I panicked!

"I swear, if you don't let me up from here."

"If I don't let you up, then what?"

"Then, I'll…"

"You won't be doing a damn thing, sweetie. I'm running this show." She laughed at my futile attempt to untie myself.

"This shit isn't funny." I continued to tug at the burlap ropes that had my arms confined to the bottom of the heating pipes.

"This isn't supposed to be funny. Well, maybe it is for me, but I'm sure you won't find any humor in this at all."

"Why are you doing this?"

"Because bitches like you deserve to lose every now and then. Now, open those legs up wide so I can take what belongs to me."

My heart rate accelerated as the liquid in the needle shot through my arm. I wanted to fight but whatever she pumped my veins with had rendered me paralyzed. "Please, stop! I don't have anything of yours. I swear it's not what you think. Please, just let me explain." Tears flew from the corners of my eyes as she continued to laugh at me. I had to admit, I had done some pretty foul things in my life but I couldn't think of any that would make someone want to do me in like this.

"I'm over wanting to hear an explanation from you. At the end of the day, you did what you did and now you must pay." Her voice took on a stern mother's tone.

"Don't do this, please. I'm begging you! I'll do whatever you want, just let me go." My pleas fell on deaf ears as she started to hum a nursery song. One I'd never heard…it seemed more sadistic than anything.

"For reasons unknown to me, you keep landing on top," she spat. "So, it's only natural that I take matters into my own hands," she whispered in my ear as I began to lose consciousness. "That's right, Tracey, take a deep breath. You never deserved to carry this precious gift, not someone as trifling as you."

Quickly, she started the tedious process of taking what she thought should've been hers in the first place. All I could do was cry and hope like hell that someone would save me. As the cramps rapidly shot through my stomach, I realized that she had come to take my baby.

IN
STORES
NOW

COMING SOON

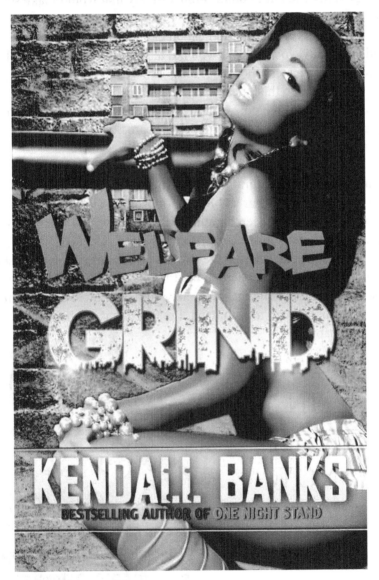

WELFARE GRIND

KENDALL BANKS

BESTSELLING AUTHOR OF ONE NIGHT STAND

V.I.P. is an explicit tale of two beautiful women both determined to become very important people 'by any means necessary'. After living in a world where you re only cool if you're the wife of an athlete, or a current T.V star they are both suddenly faced with jealousy and lies. Neither realize ...fame comes with a high, and sometimes deadly price tag. Meet India, the star struck, money hungry honey from Brooklyn, who's dead set on marrying someone well-known....even if she has to steal him from her good friend. In comes Royce, a tantalizing, sexy singer who s searching for fame in all the wrong places. Soon her past catches up with her and things spiral out of control. By hook, crook, or the good book, one of these ladies will fall hard. If you think you love Basketball Wives, hold onto your seat...V.I.P will blow your mind.

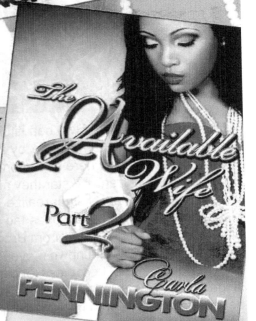

IN STORES
NOW

PICK UP
YOUR COPY
TODAY!!

LCB BOOK TITLES

MAIL TO:
PO Box 423
Brandywine, MD 20613
301-362-6508

FAX TO:
301-579-9913

ORDER FORM

Ship to:	
Address:	
City & State:	Zip:

Date:	Phone:
Email:	

Make all money orders and cashiers checks payable to: **Life Changing Books**

Qty.	ISBN	Title	Release Date	Price
	0-9741394-2-4	Bruised by Azarel	Jul-05	$ 15.00
	0-9741394-7-5	Bruised 2: The Ultimate Revenge by Azarel	Oct-06	$ 15.00
	0-9741394-3-2	Secrets of a Housewife by J. Tremble	Feb-06	$ 15.00
	0-9741394-6-7	The Millionaire Mistress by Tiphani	Nov-06	$ 15.00
	1-934230-99-5	More Secrets More Lies by J. Tremble	Feb-07	$ 15.00
	1-934230-95-2	A Private Affair by Mike Warren	May-07	$ 15.00
	1-934230-93-6	Deep by Danette Majette	Jul-07	$ 15.00
	1-934230-96-0	Flexin & Sexin Volume 1	Jun-07	$ 15.00
	1-934230-89-8	Still a Mistress by Tiphani	Nov-07	$ 15.00
	1-934230-91-X	Daddy's House by Azarel	Nov-07	$ 15.00
	1-934230-88-X	Naughty Little Angel by J. Tremble	Feb-08	$ 15.00
	1-934230847	In Those Jeans by Chantel Jolie	Jun-08	$ 15.00
	1-934230820	Rich Girls by Kendall Banks	Oct-08	$ 15.00
	1-934230839	Expensive Taste by Tiphani	Nov-08	$ 15.00
	1-934230782	Brooklyn Brothel by C. Stecko	Jan-09	$ 15.00
	1-934230669	Good Girl Gone bad by Danette Majette	Mar-09	$ 15.00
	1-934230804	From Hood to Hollywood by Sasha Raye	Mar-09	$ 15.00
	1-934230707	Sweet Swagger by Mike Warren	Jun-09	$ 15.00
	1-934230677	Carbon Copy by Azarel	Jul-09	$ 15.00
	1-934230723	Millionaire Mistress 3 by Tiphani	Nov-09	$ 15.00
	1-934230715	A Woman Scorned by Ericka Williams	Nov-09	$ 15.00
	1-934230685	My Man Her Son by J. Tremble	Feb-10	$ 15.00
	1-924230731	Love Heist by Jackie D.	Mar-10	$ 15.00
	1-934230812	Flexin & Sexin Volume 2	Apr-10	$ 15.00
	1-934230748	The Dirty Divorce by Miss KP	May-10	$ 15.00
	1-934230758	Chedda Boyz by CJ Hudson	Jul-10	$ 15.00
	1-934230766	Snitch by VegasClarke	Oct-10	$ 15.00
	1-934230693	Money Maker by Tonya Ridley	Oct-10	$ 15.00
	1-934230774	The Dirty Divorce Part 2 by Miss KP	Nov-10	$ 15.00
	1-934230170	The Available Wife by Carla Pennington	Jan-11	$ 15.00
	1-934230774	One Night Stand by Kendall Banks	Feb-11	$ 15.00
	1-934230278	Bitter by Danette Majette	Feb-11	$ 15.00
	1-934230299	Married to a Balla by Jackie D.	May-11	$ 15.00
	1-934230308	The Dirty Divorce Part 3 by Miss KP	Jun-11	$ 15.00
	1-934230316	Next Door Nympho By CJ Hudson	Jun-11	$ 15.00
	1-934230286	Bedroom Gangsta by J. Tremble	Sep-11	$ 15.00
	1-934230340	Another One Night Stand by Kendall Banks	Oct-11	$ 15.00
	1-934230359	The Available Wife Part 2 by Carla Pennington	Nov-11	$ 15.00
			Total for Books	$
		Shipping Charges (add $4.95 for 1-4 books*)		$
			Total Enclosed (add lines)	$

* Prison Orders- Please allow up to three (3) weeks for delivery.

Please Note: We are not held responsible for returned prison orders. Make sure the facility will receive books before ordering.

*Shipping and Handling of 5-10 books is $6.95, please contact us if your order is more than 10 books. (301)362-6508

CPSIA information can be obtained at www.ICGtesting.com
Printed in the USA
LVOW04s1443310814

401739LV00017B/604/P